Praise for Ed Briant's first novel,

Choppy Socky Blues

"In a field of fine coming-of-age novels for girls, here's one that boys will get a kick out of."

—*Kirkus Reviews*

"[Jason is] the kind of awkward hero readers will be glad to see come into his own."

—*Publishers Weekly*

"The pacing is right, the characters are interesting, and the plot is engaging. Its creative plot and interesting cast of characters will keep teens reading, and even capture boys' attention."

—*VOYA*

I AM
(NOT) THE
WALRUS

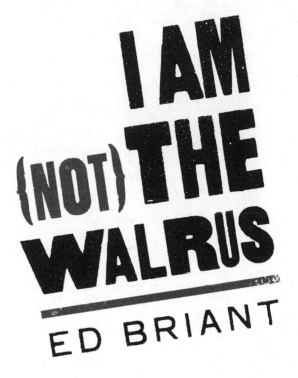

I AM (NOT) THE WALRUS

ED BRIANT

flux
™
Woodbury, Minnesota

First Edition
First Printing, 2012

Book design by Bob Gaul
Cover design by Ellen Lawson
Cover images: Guitars © iStockphoto.com/Leontura
　　　　　　　Silhouettes © iStockphoto.com/Igor Djurovic

Flux, an imprint of Llewellyn Worldwide Ltd.

Library of Congress Cataloging-in-Publication Data
Briant, Ed.
　I am (not) the walrus/Ed Briant.—1st ed.
　　p. cm.
　Summary: As the singer and bass player for a Beatles cover band, Toby embarks on a quest to increase his sex appeal, a plan that derails when he finds a mysterious note inside his old bass guitar.
　ISBN 978-0-7387-3246-6
　[1. Bands (Music)—Fiction.]　I. Title.
　PZ7.B75883Iam 2012
　[Fic]—dc23

　　　　　　　　　　　　　　　　　　　　　　2012004314

Flux
Llewellyn Worldwide Ltd.
2143 Wooddale Drive
Woodbury, MN 55125-2989
www.fluxnow.com

Printed in the United States of America

1
WEDNESDAY

Horoscope: April 14, Aquarius:

Wear something nice today as you may well find
yourself in the middle of a group of friendly
people. Even if you have nothing to say, you will
be warmly welcomed. Lasting relationships will
be formed in a moment.

Frosty lowers his head like an offended buffalo, then blows a long blast on the whistle for kickoff. Even though it's a loud peep, it's swallowed up by the sudden gust that blows in off the ocean. The wind flattens the grass, blasts up inside my rugby shorts, and rocks the trees along the edge of the playing field.

"Hey, Toby." A familiar voice from just behind me. "Your lace is undone."

"Zack! I didn't know you were here." I look down at

my laces, meandering across the grass, then over my shoulder at my friend. "Bloody things never stay fastened."

"Last-minute substitute," says Zack, in what looks like a brand-new blue shirt. "Ka-chang!" He strums an air guitar. "Hey, guess what?"

"Silence for the kickoff," yells Clive Wadman, the team captain.

"Who's talking?" barks Frosty.

Twenty yards in front of me, on the other side of the halfway line, Jasper Hamilton-Sinclair pushes up the sleeves of his red shirt, exposing arms that are bigger than my legs. He holds up a finger to test the wind, then launches himself toward the ball.

"I'm not sure this is the ideal moment for guess what," I say to Zack. "I think I have about three seconds." I drop to my knee, gather the ends of my laces, then glance up just in time to see Jasper Hamilton-Sinclair swing back a treelike leg, and boot the ball skyward. "I don't know," I say. "You're getting married."

"Nah, you bunghole," says Zack, shuffling from one foot to the other. "I'll give you a clue. We're going to have to think of a name."

"A name?" I study the trajectory of the ball as it arcs upward. It brushes the bottom of a low cloud, hovers for an instant, then begins its descent toward the right-hand side of the field. I've only played this game a couple of times before, but I think this means that the ball isn't heading in my direction.

With lightning-fast moves, I twist my laces into a knot just as another blast of wind knocks me sideways. "Are you telling me you're pregnant?"

"Nope," he says, then opens his eyes wide and points at a spot just in front of me. "Heads up, Toby!"

I spring to my feet just in time for a brown object, about the size of a small wombat, to slap into my hands.

I take a second to examine the object.

It is a rugby ball. Why would anyone bring a second rugby ball onto the pitch? As I think I mentioned, I am no expert at this game, but I thought it was supposed to be played with one ball.

There's just enough time for it to dawn on me that there is only one ball, and this is it, before Jasper Hamilton-Sinclair grasps the collar of my shirt. He lifts me right off the earth's surface, swings me around, then slams me back into the mud.

Lights flash as I gaze up at the stratocumulus clouds and listen to the thunder of boots drifting away toward our goal area.

"We need a name for the band, Toby," says Zack, "and we need it pronto."

I take a moment to examine my once-blue shirt, which is now brown, and look up to see Zack shuffling away from me toward the rest of the pack.

"Pronto?" I haul myself onto my hands and knees. "Wait. You don't mean—"

"I do mean," he says, hopping sideways. "We have a gig."

"Get out of town!" I spring into a sitting position. I scan the oddball group of spectators along the sideline. My stomach knots. Right at the end are two girls. One of them is tall and blonde, and looks a lot like my ex-girlfriend, Katrina.

I squeeze my eyes shut and shake my head. I always think every tall blonde girl is Katrina.

Besides, why in God's name would Katrina be watching an under-seventeens rugby match?

Come to think of it, why would any girls be watching a rugby match?

For a punishment?

For a dare?

Probably Jasper Hamilton-Sinclair's fan club.

Oh well, even if she's not Katrina I'd still better make this look good.

"Hang on a minute." I roll back onto my feet and stumble after Zack. "How did you manage to swing a gig?" I say when I catch up with him.

"My wit, charm," Zack steps over a red winger who's lying in a fetal position, "and winning ways." He mimes a drum roll and cymbal crash—Ba-ta-ta-ching! "Thank you!"

"Mark a man," yells Clive Wadman.

Frosty blows his whistle again, and raises his right arm. It's a set scrum.

Steve Parsons and Gregg Lester throw their arms around my shoulders, lift me off the ground, and then the three of us lower our heads and slam into the red front row. The second row lock their heads between our hips, then finally we're joined by the number eight, and the flankers, of which Zack is one. It's dark in here. And smelly. But on the plus side, it is out of the wind.

"When did this all come about?" The side of my head presses against the ear of one of the red prop forwards, and for a second our ears are like two suction cups. "Why didn't you say something earlier?"

"I only found out at lunchtime," says Zack, through the grunts and gasps. "I was down at Harry's trying out one of the new guitars he's got in, when Harry himself runs up the stairs and goes, 'Sounds good. You still in a band?' I go, 'As a matter of fact I am,' and he goes, 'What sort of stuff do you play?' So I go, 'We do cover versions of Beatles songs,' and he says, 'You want to play a support gig?' I go 'Yeah, I suppose. Why not?' And he says, 'Don't go overboard with the enthusiasm.'"

"Silence in the scrum," yells Clive Wadman.

"Who's talking in the scrum," barks Frosty. "Be quiet and concentrate."

The whistle blows, and the ball rolls in. This is my moment. I lash out, and get my foot around the ball, but at almost the same moment Paul Hammerton, the red hooker, lashes out and kicks me right on the shin. Pain sears up my leg.

"Heave!" shouts Clive Wadman.

"Push," barks Frosty. "What are you? Men? Or mice?"

"Squeak, squeak," goes someone behind me.

The scrum lurches forward. I kick out and get my foot

on top of the ball, but the other dude kicks it out from underneath me again, and it's in the reds' possession. The air is filled with shouts. Once again I'm in daylight, and once again we're stumbling backward toward our own goal.

I almost trip over Steve Agar, who's on his hands and knees, then catch up with Zack. We struggle to make a defensive line. "So, who are we opening for?" I say.

Once again the ball slaps into my hands.

"Move it out," shouts Clive Wadman.

"Play up!" barks Frosty.

Fine. I turn. I'm just about to throw the ball to a player with a blue shirt, when I realize that the player is Zack, so I turn to pass it to the other side. My hands strike something that feels more like concrete than a person. It's neither a red shirt, nor a blue shirt. It's a tweed jacket.

"Pull yourself together, you scallywag," yells Frosty as he swipes the ball out of my hands. He tucks his head down. "This is what you need to do." He lays into the red forwards with his leather-patched elbows. Even Jasper Hamilton-Sinclair staggers backward with a look of horror, as if Frosty really is a charging buffalo.

"What did Frosty do before he was a teacher?" I say, over my shoulder.

"He was a Commando, or a Marine." Zack points at the other team. "Or something like that. He probably thinks they're Germans."

"Pretty impressive," I say as Frosty is swallowed up into the mob. "He's got to be fifty years old or something."

"Anyway." Zack slaps me across the back. "We're supporting the Disappointed Parents. Harry's band."

"The Disappointed Parents!" I turn and grab two handfuls of Zack's shirt. "They're famous!"

"Well..." Zack straightens out his lapels as if he's wearing a fancy dinner suit instead of a rugby shirt. "They're famous in Port Jackson at any rate."

"I wouldn't mind being famous in Port Jackson," I say.

Red players rush past us, putting us offside, so we jog backward. I'm getting good at the running backward part of this game.

"Listen," says Zack. "You have to do something about your bass guitar."

"What do you mean?" I say.

Zack speeds up so I almost have to break into a sprint to get in front of him.

"I think you should take it down to Harry's and trade it in for another one," he says. "Something is seriously wrong with it."

Another whistle. "Line out," shouts a red player.

We arrange ourselves, puffing and panting, in order of height at the touch-line, the tallest players in the middle. This leaves me at one end of the line, and Zack at the other, us being about the shortest players on the field.

"But it's not my bass to trade," I say, in between gasps for air. "Shawn's letting us use all his stuff out of the goodness of his heart. It's a bit inconsiderate to repay his kindness by selling his bass."

"Silence in the line," yells Clive Wadman.

"Who's talking in the line?" barks Frosty. He jerks his head from side to side, then blows the whistle yet again.

The ball flies up. We all jump, but a red player gets his hands on it. The ball makes its way out to the fast runners on the red wing, and the blue defense falls apart.

"Look. I think I can fix it," I say to Zack. "Shawn has a soldering iron somewhere."

"Can you do it this evening?" he says. "If we're going to play a gig then we can't have it making crackling noises and cutting out in the middle of the songs, or maybe even completely self-destructing."

"Yeah. I know what you mean," I say. "The bass does seem to have a mind of its own. It always seems to go on the blink at the worst possible moment."

"Bummer," says Zack, as the red winger crosses our twenty-five yard line, with the ball securely tucked into his armpit. "Looks like we're going to lose again."

I make a lame attempt to tuck my shirt into my shorts. "I'll do it this weekend, though. Be easier to solder in daylight."

"No. No!" says Zack. "You can't do it tomorrow. Do it tonight. I mean, how can we rehearse a set if one of the instruments isn't working?"

"Fantastic," I say. I slide my hands into the pockets of my shorts. "No pressure."

A large person in a red shirt appears in front of us. It

is Jasper Hamilton-Sinclair, his fingers wrapped around the ball.

"Would you mind taking that thing somewhere else," says Zack, pointing at the ball.

"Just taking it to your goal line," says Jasper Hamilton-Sinclair. "Seemed like the easy route would be via you two big-girls'-blouses." With that, he shoves his free hand into Zack's face and sends him sprawling.

Then he turns toward me.

"Look at you," he says. "Pathetic. If your brother could see you now he would weep in shame."

The moment he says this something flickers in the corner of my eye, like someone switching channels on a TV, and there, standing in his navy uniform with his arms folded, is my brother, Shawn. He puffs his cheeks and blows out a long breath of exasperation.

A split second later he's gone and all I can see is a red shirt. Jasper Hamilton-Sinclair's hand shoots up toward my face. I flex my knees and slip under his arm. I lunge forward, butt my head into his six pack as hard as I can, then lock my hands around his waist. There's no way he can punch me in the face now; instead he hammers on the back of my skull with the ball. I hang on for dear life as I let myself drop, and then squeeze his knees together.

At first nothing happens, and I ponder the fact that I may already be dead. Then the light shifts as Jasper Hamilton-Sinclair's upper body continues to move forward, while his boots remain anchored, by my arms, to one square foot of turf. A moment later the ground shudders, and there is a howl so profound that it might come from the earth's crust itself.

I lie there gazing up at the cumulonimbus from between Jasper Hamilton-Sinclair's hairy legs. I roll them to one side, and rise to my feet. Jasper Hamilton-Sinclair is stretched out right in front of our goal line. The ball rolls over the line.

"Oh well," I say to Zack. "They won. Let's go and play some music."

"No," says Zack. "In rugby, the player has to cross the goal line, and also touch the ball to the ground to score." He points to Jasper Hamilton-Sinclair. "He's only dropped the ball across the line. It doesn't count."

"Play on!" bellows Frosty. "What is this? You look like a bunch of grannies at a Sunday-school picnic."

I study Zack for a moment, then I study the ball. Why is nobody doing anything? Red and blue players are arranged around us in a semi-circle, as if they're taking part in a pageant.

Then, off in the distance, I notice the two girls on the touch-line.

They are not merely watching the game.

They are watching me.

They are watching me while I do nothing.

"Bugger this." I scoop up the ball, turn my back on our goal, and stumble into a steady run.

What the hell. Nobody lives forever.

Any second I expect to be flattened into the turf. I expect to be buried, to have grass planted on top of me, and to have generations of happy children playing tag above me. But nothing happens. Blue players stagger back to let me through. Red players stand in my path, but then melt away as I get closer.

A blast of wind hits me square in the face, almost bringing me to a standstill. I look up. Nobody is between me and the red goal. I tuck my head down and force my way into the wind. My feet fly over the rutted grass as an unfastened bootlace whips around my ankles. I glance at the sideline, and for a moment I seem to be standing still as the motley mob of spectators blur past me.

I never realized a rugby pitch was so long. I reach out imaginary tendrils from my forehead and wrap them around the goal posts, but they still don't get any closer. Every second I expect to feel the grip of hands around my shoulders, sharp nails digging into my back, mighty fingers pulling my hair out of my scalp.

Then I'm alongside the last two spectators. It's worse than I thought.

Not only are they girls.

Not only are they around my age.

They're pretty. A tall blonde one and a shorter dark-haired one.

Dammit. I'm going to score if it kills me.

The goal line is three paces away, then two paces, then one. And then I slam into the ground. The ball bounces forward. My fingertips are three inches away from the line. No. I scored. Surely I won the game? But the whistle blows.

I roll over and gaze at my feet. My shoelaces are twisted around both of my ankles in a granny knot.

"Ball thrown forward," barks Frosty. "Offside."

I roll back and glance over at the two girls. They look away from me. Presumably from a sense of shame.

Oh well. It's not the end of the world.

Even if I had scored a goal, they still would have been way out of my league.

2
WEDNESDAY

"How about the Zack Lawrence Experience for a name?" says Zack as we exit the school gate. The green man is blinking on the pedestrian signal, so we cross straight to the opposite side of Portland Road. I always feel more relaxed when I have a four-lane road between me and school.

"Zack Lawrence?" I say. "Why not the Toby Holland Experience?"

"Let me ask you this." Zack leans his guitar case against a crooked lamp post. "Would you pay good money to see the Toby Holland Experience?" Engines roar as the pedestrian signal changes, and the traffic takes off like it's the start of a Grand Prix race.

"Would you pay anything at all to see the Zack Lawrence Experience?" I say. A van clatters past with a dog hanging out of the window. "Why don't we use both our names, Holland and Lawrence?"

"Sounds more like a hemorrhoid ointment than a pop group," Zack growls. "Quick. Run out and get me a tube of Holland and Lawrence." He pulls his little round John Lennon glasses out of his jacket pocket, and props them on his nose. "If our whole set is Beatles songs, then maybe we should do something with a Beatles reference."

"Hey listen. What do you want to do now?" I point at his guitar case. "Seems like we should run through some new songs."

"Nah. You're right," says Zack. He plays a couple of chords on his air guitar, ba-chang!

"We should get cracking then," I say. "After we play I've got to do the soldering on the bass, and then read four chapters of *Fahrenheit 451*."

"Yeah. I'm supposed to be writing to Bethany later on anyway." Zack picks up his guitar case and rests it on his shoulder like it's a rifle. "Lead the way, Batman."

We march westward along Portland Road. Only a line of parked cars separates us from the endless stream of traffic hurtling in the opposite direction, as if they know something we don't.

"How about the Paperback Writers?" I say.

"It's not bad," says Zack, "but I don't think we can just name ourselves after a Beatles song title."

A squeal of tires makes me turn. A black car peels out of its parking spot just behind us, and slots into the eastbound traffic.

"John, Paul, Zack, and Toby," I say.

Zack blows out his cheeks. "I like it," he says. "But it's a bit weird if there's only two of us."

"It's surreal," I say.

We move to opposite sides of the pavement so a mom with a double stroller can pass us.

I shove my hands in my pockets. "The Beatles did a lot of surreal stuff."

"Cereal?" says Zack. "Like breakfast cereal?"

"Surreal, like Salvador Dalí," I say.

"Like sitting on a cornflake," says Zack.

"Whoa," I say. "That went over my head,"

"It's a line from 'I Am The Walrus,'" says Zack.

"We don't do 'I Am The Walrus,'" I say.

"Maybe we should." Zack stops and turns around to look at the mom with the stroller. "I think I'm getting old."

"With just the two of us?" I walk on a couple of paces, then stop. "Me doing bass and vocals, and you on guitar? I think that particular song needs an entire orchestra."

"We should try it," says Zack, rubbing his chin absentmindedly. "You never know."

"What? Just so we can call ourselves Sitting on a

Cornflake?" I take a couple of paces back. "What makes you think you're getting old?"

Zack is still rubbing his chin. "I'm starting to find young mums attractive," he says.

"Come on." I start walking backward. "We need to get going."

Zack continues to watch the departing mom for a moment, then seems to have to wrench himself away. "Didn't you think she was pretty?" he says as he catches up with me.

"To be honest, I didn't really look," I say. "I was trying to think of names."

"Toby. I can't believe you," he says. "A woman like that passes you in the street and you don't even notice. I mean she was gorgeous."

"Okay," I say. "Maybe I did look for a second, and she looked nice, but I mean, what's the point in working myself up into a frenzy of desire? Firstly, she's married, and secondly, a female that pretty is never even going to look at a dude like me."

"First," says Zack, "you don't know that she's married, and second, I bet that if you just smiled and said hello she would melt into your arms."

"I wouldn't bet on it," I say.

"Bet?" says Zack. "Yeah, I'll put a bet on it. The next pretty girl we see, you just smile and say hello and she'll smile back."

"Wait a minute," I say. "What are we betting?"

"If she smiles and says hello," says Zack, "then we call the band Sitting on a Cornflake."

"Fine," I say. "I think I'm completely safe there. You are bound to lose."

We both stop at the curb to let a van pass.

"We'll see," says Zack. He steps off the curb and scuffs his feet as he crosses the asphalt of Maple Street.

I shove my hands into my pockets and look toward Memento Park and the big monument of the World War II pilot. There's a dark silhouette on top of the monument. I don't even see it until it moves. For a second I think it's a cat, but then it lifts its wings.

I don't know much about birds. In fact, I don't really know a lot about animals. I used to try to watch nature programs on the TV, but Mom always seemed to come in just as the rhinos were having sex. Anyway, I can't take my eyes away from this particular bird, and as I stare I can see that it is kind of blue-gray, but with a black-and-white striped stomach. It's not so much that it's big, but more that it's wide, a little like a pigeon that's been lifting weights. As I watch, the bird shuffles forward and steps into space. It plummets straight down the front of the monument. My insides lurch. Is this bird going to kill itself right in front of me? But just before it hits the concrete, it splays its wings and shoots forward, parallel to the ground, straight toward me. A moment later it rockets over my head, giving me a clear view of its striped underside and two eyes staring at me like tiny lasers.

"Zack." I reach over and grab his arm. "Look."

But Zack isn't paying any attention. "Bingo," he says.

His gaze is focused on the other side of the street. I follow his eyes. Two girls are headed toward us on the opposite side of Portland Road. Unless I'm very mistaken, they're the ones who were watching the rugby game.

I glance overhead and scan the skyline, but there's no sign of the bird. So much for that.

I look back at the girls.

They're talking loudly as they walk.

I can hear their voices, but not loudly enough that I can make out what they're saying. The one farthest away from us is tall and very thin, with light blonde hair. She's walking with her arms folded. As for the girl nearest to us, she's facing away from us so I can't see her face, but she's much shorter than the blonde one, not so thin, and has darker hair. It must be an important conversation from the way she's waving her arms about.

"There you go," says Zack.

"What do you expect me to do?" I say. "Just walk over there and say hi?"

"Exactly," says Zack.

"But there's two of them," I say. "Which one do I say hi to?"

"Whichever one you want." Zack comes to a full stop and turns to face me. The expression on his face sends chills down my arms. It's a little like that movie, *Psycho*, where the detective spins the old lady's chair around, and it turns out to be a skeleton wearing a wig and a dress. Only in this case, the shock comes from seeing Zack being completely sincere.

"But we haven't got time now," I say. I walk past Zack in the direction of my house, but he makes no move to follow. "We have to go and rehearse, remember?" I wave my hands in front of his face. "I have to fix the electrics on my bass, and then we have a gig in just five days."

"Toby." Zack shakes his head. "I can't believe I have to tell you this, but the whole point of playing rock and roll is to make yourself more interesting to girls." He puts his guitar case down and shoves his hands into his pockets, as if to emphasize the fact that he is not going to move. "If you have to pass up an opportunity for romance in order to work on your set, then you're not just barking up the wrong tree, you're barking in the wrong bloody forest." Zack turns and studies the girls. The shorter one still has her back to us. "If not merely barking mad."

"Point taken," I say, "but now is not the time."

"When it comes to love, my friend," says Zack, patting his chest, "now is always the time." He waves me back to where he's standing. "You are going to cross the street and talk to them."

"On my own?" I glance across the street. I have never seen such scary-looking girls. I would rather try to strike up a conversation with a pack of hyenas. "There's two. Why don't you come as well?"

"But I already have a girlfriend," says Zack. "What if Bethany found out?"

"How's she going to find out if she's in Norway, for God's sake?" I turn my back on the girls and face homeward. "Anyway, it's beside the point," I say. "Let's just go and play some music."

"Look. Get over there." Zack grabs my shoulders and spins me back to face them. "Remember the time you stood on the edge of the top diving board and you couldn't jump, and then you did jump, and it was fun?"

"I didn't jump," I say. "I climbed back down the ladder."

"Well, there's no ladder this time, Toby," he says. "Just do it."

"All right," I say. "All right." I let a bus pass by, then step off the curb and look both ways. I'm going to need to cross at a forty-five degree angle. A red VW is heading toward me, but it's far enough away that I'll be across before it gets here. I mutter silently to myself as I cross.

They are just girls. They will not do me any physical harm. By the time I'm halfway across, I've halfway convinced myself. I fine-tune my trajectory so I will arrive at the opposite curb about ten yards ahead of them.

I'm so close now that I can eavesdrop on their conversation, and at that moment it strikes me that I have no idea what I'm going to say to them. I need to focus on what they're talking about.

"Eight out of ten," says the shorter one, still turned away from me.

They must be talking about the results they got for a test.

"I don't know," says the tall one. "Seven at the very best." She catches sight of me, and furrows her brows as if she knows exactly what my plans are.

"How about seven and a half?" says the shorter one.

"Well, that's half a point for charity." The taller one keeps her eyes on me, then the shorter one turns. I freeze mid-stride. She has eyes so big she almost looks like a manga character. She shakes her head from side to side. *No,* she seems to be saying, *Not a good idea.*

I am in complete agreement, and I'm about to beat a retreat when a car honks. I swivel to the left, just in time to see the VW hurtling toward me. It's going much faster than I've ever seen anything move on Portland Road, and the driver has no intention of swerving out of my way.

Bastard!

Without looking, or even thinking, I lunge forward and flatten myself against the door of a parked car. I spin around just as the VW passes. The gust of wind rips my shirt out of my waistband. The car doesn't slow, or even swerve. I try to see the driver, but all I get is a glimpse of a bony fist gripping the steering wheel. "Bloody lunatic!" I shout.

With my chest pounding, I stagger backward to the pavement, trying to get a look at the license plate. I lift my foot, but I trip over the curb. As I turn, I instinctively reach out for something to break my fall—a slender pair of shoulders wrapped in a soft, blue sweater.

It's not quite the tackle I did on Jasper Hamilton-Sinclair, but it slams the shorter girl into her tall friend.

"Bloody hell," I cry. "I'm sorry. I'm so sorry. Are you okay?"

She recovers her balance and turns on me. Her eyes, which were already about twice the size of a normal human's, now cover about two-thirds of the surface of her face. Even so, I think I see the ghost of a sympathetic smile. It's all going to work out. Zack was right after all.

"What are you? Five years old?" she says. Her face turns from peach to brick-red. "Why don't you sodding well grow up?"

Blood pounds into my cheeks as well. "It wasn't my fault," I say. I point to the street. "It was that car!"

The taller girl straightens her top. "Shelly, are you okay?"

Now both of them glare at me.

"We were just giving scores out of ten to all the boys we know." The shorter one rolls her shoulder as if it's gone stiff. "I think I'm going to give you nought out of ten."

"The car," I say, waving my hand at the street. "Didn't you see the car?"

"Oh, come on, Shelly," says the taller one. "I know he's a total clown, but you could give him one out of ten."

"It was going at ninety miles an hour!" I say. "I'm sorry."

"Nope," says Shelly. "Nought out of ten."

"We need to go." The taller girl pulls on Shelly's sleeve. "Give him a half a point out of ten."

"No. Nothing. Zilch. Bugger all." Shelly glares at me

for a moment as if she's about to say something more, then she swivels and follows her friend.

"But the car," I say to their departing backs. "Didn't you see the car?"

They don't turn around.

"I guess that's the end of Sitting on a Cornflake," says Zack. He must have snuck across the street without my noticing. As he steps up onto the curb he pretends to stumble. "We could call ourselves the Day Trippers."

"Very funny," I say.

I look back at the two girls. They stopped about half a block away, and are chatting with an older woman. All three of them turn and scowl at me at the same time. "Let's get out of here," I say.

3
WEDNESDAY

Up in Shawn's room I plug Shawn's bass into Shawn's amp.

"Why don't we run through 'Ticket to Ride'?" says Zack. He lifts his guitar out of its case and strums a couple of chords to test the tuning. "She was pretty nice, actually."

If it hadn't been for my brother, Shawn, being in the Indian Ocean, and blowing his Navy pay-packet on a ton of musical equipment that he hardly ever used, then the band would not have existed.

"Good idea." I perch on the edge of Shawn's bed, place Shawn's Beatles's Fake Book by my feet, then flick through the pages until I find "Ticket to Ride." "Who was pretty nice, actually?" I say as I scan through the chords.

There's a hum as Zack plugs his guitar in. Zack's guitar is just about the only thing we use that isn't Shawn's, but he still has to plug it into Shawn's amp so we can hear it.

"Your little friend from earlier," says Zack. His guitar pings as he tests the harmonics. "You know, the one you bumped into on Portland Road."

"Ha. Bumped into. Very funny. She was pretty, I'll give you that." I turn the tuning keys of the bass and strain to hear the tell-tale throb that lets me know I'm in tune. "She doesn't seem to have the most civil way of communicating, though."

"Pretty face and a potty mouth," says Zack as he twiddles his machine heads. "Some people find that quite disarming."

"Oh, no. I didn't mean rude in a sexy way." I place the open book at my feet where I can see the words and play at the same time. "I meant more in a personally insulting kind of way."

"That's too bad." Zack plucks an "E" harmonic. The high-pitched ping hovers over our heads like the magic "E" fairy who has to attend all occasions where two or more guitarists come together. "I thought you two were getting on like a house on fire."

"More like a house of pain," I say. "Come on. Let's play."

Zack uses one of Shawn's pens to scrawl the guitar chords onto a napkin, which he then props on the amp where he can see it. He could have used the music stand but, as he's often pointed out, music stands are not rock and roll.

"You fit?" he says.

"Close enough for jazz," I say. "Let's run through a couple of choruses without the vocals." I tap my foot to get the rhythm. "One … two … three … four … " The song lumbers into motion. It sounds like a dirge, so I up the tempo. Zack catches up with me, and then shoots ahead, but by the time we get to the end of the first chorus it's starting to rock, and as the end of the second chorus approaches, it's beginning to sound fairly presentable. Now it gets tricky, because in order for it to be something we can play at the audition we have to add the vocals.

Playing a musical instrument and singing at the same time is no simple matter. A lot of people have compared it to patting your head while you rub your stomach. Playing and singing in harmony is even trickier, and I count down the beats to the start of the vocals as if I'm about to start riding my skateboard down a flight of stairs while juggling chain saws.

I clear my throat, take a long breath, and nod to Zack. We mouth the first "I" in perfect timing, then I get my tongue twisted around "think," Zack misses a beat, and then I get the tingle in the back of my neck. The surge of electricity that lets me know it's all working, and once it's working everything seems to slot into place, and it's almost like it's better not to try to think too hard about it, but just let the music almost play itself.

Trouble with letting the music play itself is that my mind tends to wander, and that's exactly what happens. One moment I'm listening to Zack play the guitar chords, I'm concentrating on the beat, and I'm plucking the strings, and then the next moment the walls of Shawn's room disappear and I'm back on Portland Road.

I step off the curb, I let the bus pass, and as the VW roars past, I hammer on the roof with the side of my fist. The VW squeals to a halt. The driver jumps out. He looks a lot like Jasper Hamilton-Sinclair. He swings a fist at me. I slip under it, slam a left hook into his ribs, then a right uppercut to his chin. He hits the front wing of his VW as he tumbles back, and somersaults over it onto the asphalt.

I dust my hands off then turn to the girls.

The taller one looks puzzled, but the shorter one just beams at me. I still can't think of anything to say, but I don't need to.

"Hiya," she says. Her smile gets even wider.

"I'll see you around," says the tall one, and just keeps walking.

"Hiya," says the shorter one again. She slides her fingertips between my arms and my ribs, then pulls me toward her.

"Hey, Toby," yells Zack.

Not now, Zack! I think.

The girl—Shelly, yes, that was her name—stands on

tiptoe, turns her face up toward mine, opens her lips, and vanishes with a loud electrical crack. At exactly the same moment my bass goes dead, and I'm back in Shawn's room as abruptly as I left it. The transition is so sudden I feel like I've been dropped through the ceiling and I have to make an effort to stay on my feet. I keep singing, and for a few beats I keep plucking the strings, even though no sound is coming out.

"Bollocks." Zack stops playing and throws his hands in the air.

Just for good measure the bass makes a final pop.

Zack shakes his head. "Come on, Toby, you have to fix that thing otherwise you're going to make us look like a couple of dingbats." He lowers his head and checks his tuning even though he's about as in tune as he can get.

I give the instrument a sharp thump with the heel of my hand, then try the strings. The notes boom out of the amplifier. "See. All better," I say to the pattern of hair on the top of Zack's head.

He looks up like a crocodile that's just spotted a wildebeest, a look that lets me know that it's anything but "all better," and as if to underline the point, the bass emits a final pop!

I jiggle the cable until the interference stops, and then I count us in again.

"Wait up, wait up," yells Zack over the boom of my bass. He reaches over and puts a hand on my strings. They go clonky-clonk with his hand damping them.

"Let's just keep going," I say. "I mean, we can live with it just for this evening. I promise I'll fix it after we finish."

"It's not so much the bass." Zack frowns. "Could you sing that last line again without the music?"

"I think I'm gonna be sad," I sing, and then I stop singing. "I'm pretty sure they're the right words?" I point to the Fake Book. "It is unofficial," I say. "I mean, the words could be completely wrong."

"No, they weren't the wrong words." Zack uses his guitar pick to tap his teeth.

"So..." I say. "Was I off-key?"

"No," says Zack, but his pained expression doesn't change. "Your voice is great. I really like the way you're even copying the Liverpool accent a bit. You almost don't sound like a cockney at all."

"Thanks," I say. "I've been working on that, but—"

"Your bass playing is fine too."

"Okay."

"I might even say it's pretty good," says Zack.

"So...?"

"There's your problem." Zack points his long index finger at my face.

Right away I think, nought out of ten.

"Are you telling me I'm too ugly to play Beatles music?" I say.

Zack shakes his head. "Blimey, mate." He gives me one of those grimaces that hair-metal guitarists pull at a climactic point of their guitar solos. "I mean if it came down to that, then we'd all be back to playing Bach minuets."

"So," I say. "What, then?"

"It's your expression," says Zack. "You just look so . . ." He glances around the room as if he's searching for the right word. "Bummed out."

I gaze down at the Fake Book by my feet. I read through the first lines of "Ticket to Ride" as if they might have a solution to this problem. I mean the Bible was once supposed to have solutions for all human problems. Maybe the Beatles's Fake Book is the new Bible. Maybe the solution to all our problems is concealed within the lyrics of the Beatles. "I have a naturally bummed-out expression," I say. "It's who I am."

"Would it kill you to smile just a little?" says Zack. "Even if it's only when we're playing in front of people."

"But it's a sad song?" I say. "See. Here." I point to the lyrics. "The first line goes 'I think I'm gonna be sad.'"

"You're going to be sad," says Zack. "You can't be going to be sad if you're already sad, and anyway you look more hostile than sad."

"Look," I say, "we have less than five days to put together a killer set. Can't we just figure out the words and the music for now? Maybe we can work on my demeanor for the next gig." I tap my foot again, but Zack unhooks his guitar strap.

"Just wait." He props the guitar against the side of the

amp. "This is important, Toby. Please just try and look a little less morose."

When Zack gets an idea in his head there is no shifting it. I'm going to have to sit this one out. I tip the bass sideways onto my legs, lean my elbows on the sound board, and stretch my mouth into a grin. "How's that?" I mutter through my teeth.

"It's like Heath Ledger playing the Joker," says Zack. "Do you have something a little less demented?"

I stretch my mouth wider.

"Better," says Zack. "But it's more like Jabba the Hutt now. Show your teeth."

I stretch my mouth so much my cheeks hurt.

"No. Now you look like you're going to bite me," says Zack. "You know what I think?"

"No," I say. "What do you think?"

"I think," says Zack, "that you spend too much time tormenting yourself over what happened with Katrina."

"Katrina! I haven't thought about Katrina for—I don't know—ages." I prop my bass back up into a playing position, thump out the descending notes that lead into the first chord, and then stop. "Look. I don't think I can deal with this right now. Let's play."

"You were thinking about her when we played rugby this afternoon." Zack picks up his guitar and puts the strap back over his shoulder.

"I was not!"

"Oh really?" says Zack points a long finger at me.

"The whole time you made that long run, you were staring at those two girls on the touch-line. You were thinking about how one of them reminded you of Katrina. That's why you tripped."

"That's completely out of order," I say.

"Then ... " Zack wags his finger. "Then you were thinking the same thing when you crossed Portland Road." He spreads his arms. "That's why you almost got hit by that car."

"That's not true," I say.

"Then just now, when we were playing, you were thinking about her," says Zack. "You've got to let go. Come to terms with rejection. Move on. She's ruining your life." He scratches his chin. "Well. To be honest, it's not Katrina who's ruining your life. It's your memory of her."

"Move on to what?" I say.

"Not all girls are like Katrina," says Zack. "That girl you bumped into isn't Katrina." Zack prods himself in the chest with his thumb. "You know what? I bet you misjudged her. I think she had a soft spot for you."

"Wait," I say, "What exactly do you think I misjudged?"

"Nothing specific," says Zack. "It's just a feeling I had. I've got to admit I'm a little jealous. She was kind of fit-looking."

"You didn't hear what she said to me," I say. "They were giving points out of ten to all the boys they knew, and she gave me nothing."

"Nothing?" says Zack.

"Correct," I say. "Zero. What part of zero out of ten are you claiming I misunderstood?"

"Nothing out of ten is better than nothing out of a hundred." Zack gives me a thousand-yard stare through one eye. Kind of a five-hundred-yard stare.

"Nothing," I say, "is zero. Zero is always zero. Zero out of ten is the same as zero out of a hundred."

"Okay, so she gave you nothing." Zack absent-mindedly thrums the opening chords to "Can't Buy Me Love."

"Not one," I say.

"Not a half?" says Zack.

"Nothing." I say.

"My opinion, for what it's worth." Zack places the end of his guitar on the floor and draws in a long, ragged breath. "If she'd given you one or two out of ten, I'd say forget it. But zero is a bit over the top." He slaps his hands on his knees. "I mean nobody is worth nothing. I reckon she was actually trying to pretend she didn't like you."

"She did a pretty good job of pretending," I say. "She convinced me."

"You don't get it, do you," says Zack. "She wasn't trying to convince you."

"Who then?" I say. "Her friend?"

Zack puts his face in his hands. "She was trying to convince herself." He puts his guitar on the bed, stands up, and goes over to the window.

"So. Fine," I say. "She's convinced herself she doesn't

like me. It's all the same in the end. Let's play." I point to his guitar.

"You don't get it do you?" Zack leans against the wall. "She needed to convince herself because she actually did like you. If you see her again, all you have to do is un-convince her."

"Ha. If I see her again," I say. "I'm going to break the world land-speed record heading in the opposite direction."

"Oh, well," says Zack. "Plenty of fish in the sea."

"Plenty of fish in the aquarium." I trace the lines of the cables as they snake across the floor like railway lines on a map. "If I want a fling with a flounder."

4
WEDNESDAY

We play until Mom comes home from work, then we pack up and Zack heads home. Back in Shawn's room, I tidy up, stack all the cables away, and then I take the p-bass back out of its case again. I sit on the bed and lay the instrument across my knees.

The first thing I try is jiggling the volume and tone controls. They're tight. So is the jack socket.

I flip the bass over. On the back of the body is an oval-shaped plastic panel, about six inches along. I hold the bass sideways. The panel is right underneath the volume and tone knobs, and it's fastened to the underside of the body with three little Phillips screws.

I hate going through Shawn's stuff, but I know he has some tools in the top drawer of his nightstand. I pull the drawer open, take the items out of the drawer one at a time, and then place them on top of the stand.

Socks, handkerchiefs, a Swiss army knife, pencils, ballpoint pens, pack of Juicy Fruit chewing gum, a lock of hair fastened with what looks like a length of shoelace, a Sandman comic, a pack of Durex condoms.

I have to stop.

I shouldn't be doing this.

There's probably a screwdriver downstairs in the kitchen or something.

The last thing I take out is a wallet. I open it up. It's empty. Not that I care. I open the drawer wider to put the wallet back, and my fingers brush against something else. Another wallet. The first one was brown leather. This one is black, and made from a kind of nylon material. I open it, and a third wallet drops out. A red one. I shove them all to the back of the drawer, and then I notice two more wallets. Another brown leather one, and a black one with a zipper. Shawn had a thing for wallets.

Who would have guessed?

Funny the things you learn.

If only he'd had a thing for screwdrivers.

I open the drawer wider and scoop everything back until I reach the Swiss army knife. I weigh it in my hand for a moment. I pull open the blades. There is no Phillips-head screwdriver blade, but there's a very narrow, normal screwdriver in the knife. I try it in one of the screws.

It fits.

I twist it.

At first the screw is stuck fast, but then it creaks and shifts to the left so suddenly that the screwdriver slips out of the screw and scrapes across the panel, leaving a tiny scratch.

Dammit! I can't get anything right.

I blow out a long, ragged breath.

I borrow Shawn's bass, and just to show my gratitude, I damage it.

As it eases counterclockwise, I wonder how long the screw has been fastened. The p-bass is at least ten years old. Fenders are well made, the electrics are good, and there's probably never been a need to undo it before now. The screw begins to turn freely, so I put down the knife and use my finger, but just as I touch the tip of my finger to the head of the screw I notice a tiny scratch, thin as a hair, and about a half-inch long, radiating out from the next screw.

I can barely suppress a sigh of relief. Not only has the panel been opened before, but whoever opened it probably also used the wrong kind of screwdriver.

I use the tip of my finger to finish unfastening the first screw, and then with great care so there are no more scratches, I use a combo of the knife and my fingertip to remove the other two. I balance the three screws on the top of the nightstand so I can put them back later. It turns out that I need the knife again, as the plastic panel is recessed into the wooden body. I hold my breath as I use the tip of the knife to pry it up.

Underneath, the body is hollowed out to make room for the drum-shaped pods connected to the volume and tone controls. There's also a little bird's nest of wires that flip upward when I take away the lid. I lean forward and blow away some old sawdust, some of which goes in my eye.

I wipe it away, and blink.

The drum-shaped pods and the wiring I understand. I've seen the same kind of thing before when we opened the back of Zack's guitar. But there's something else I'm not familiar with. Under the cables is a pale-blue tube, more or less the exact size and shape of my little finger. I use the knife blade to poke the tube, and it squashes easily.

I'm just about to prod it again when something scuttles across the floor. I freeze with the knife blade a fraction of an inch above the tube.

A mouse?

A moth?

Just my imagination?

No. That's crazy. There really was something there.

It's so quiet that the loudest thing is my breathing, so I hold my breath. I can hear the faint clatter of plates downstairs as Mom makes supper. I can hear seagulls squawking outside the window. I can hear the distant rumble of traffic on the bypass. But nothing more from inside the room. Whatever it was stays put.

I breathe out, lower the knife blade back into the wiring, and test all of the connections. Apart from one wire, which has now come completely adrift, the rest of the soldering all seems to be pretty sound. The one connection that is adrift is the one that is holding down the little tube.

Why would Fender put a tube under a wire that would create enough pressure to break the connection?

But even as I put the thought together in my head, I know that I'm wrong. It's not a design fault of the guitar. The blue tube has nothing to do with the guitar. It was put in by some previous owner long after the guitar was made. Maybe even the person who used the wrong kind of knife and scratched the panel.

Now the question is, why would someone put this tube into the electrics?

Was it some kind of modification to improve the sound?

The Swiss army knife has a set of tweezers. Once again I hold my breath and use the tweezers to finagle the tube out from under the wires, without breaking any more connections.

I swallow hard. As the tube comes free I realize what it is. At almost exactly the same moment there's another flash of movement on the floor and I drop the knife into the wiring. With shaking fingers, I fish out the knife, then once again use the tweezers and draw the tube free from the wires.

I can just make out faint blue lines.

It is a rolled up Post-it note, a couple of inches square, held into a tube shape by the sticky strip.

A message in a bottle, except that it's a message in a p-bass.

A draft of icy air wafts in through the window.

I wish I'd put on a sweater before I started on this escapade, but I'm too curious to get to the bottom of it to stop now. When the note was put in here, it was probably bright blue, but now it has faded and yellowed with age. When I was in primary school we made white paper turn yellow by leaving it on a sunny windowsill. It took a couple of days. We put blocks on the paper, and under the blocks the paper remained white. I don't know how long it would take a piece of blue paper to fade, sealed up in the innards of a bass.

The sun has set, and Shawn's room is almost totally dark. I lower the bass onto the bed beside me, move close to the nightstand, and flick on the desk lamp.

A hollow feeling spreads across my chest as I unroll the paper. The faded script reads:

PLEASE. If you find this note inside the bass, then the instrument has been stolen. Please, please, please, return it to me as soon as you can. This instrument is everything to me, and without it my entire existence will be meaningless. I am Julie McGuire, 48B Mariner Street, Brunswick, BK57SA, Tel: 554553. I am

prepared give you a reward of two hundred pounds,
no questions asked.—Kisses, Julie.

All of the letters' "I's" have little circles over them, apart from the "I" of Julie, which has a little heart over it. A sort of numbness runs down the underside of my arms. I turn the note over. Nothing is on the back.

I hold it up in front of the lamp so the glow of the bulb shines through it, but nothing more is there. I close my eyes. Maybe I'm hoping that when I open them, the note will have vanished. Just an illusion.

But it is still there.

I return my attention to the little hollow on the back of the bass. I hold the body of the instrument under the light and tip it back and forth to get a better look inside, then I freeze.

Whatever it is scoots across the floor again. I take long, steady breaths as I tip the desk lamp up and cast the beam over to the other side of the room.

I shake my head.

Nothing.

What was I thinking?

That the bass was haunted?

I lay the bass on Shawn's bed, then turn my attention back to the note. Even though the script swims in front of my eyes, I can still see that each letter is big and carefully rounded.

It's nice handwriting. Much better than my own. I've

never really thought about analyzing anyone's handwriting before, but the way this is written I can almost see this Julie person's hand as it moves across the page.

I look across at the bass lying next to me. I can see her fingers moving across the strings. What am I supposed to do? Should I follow the instructions in the note and give it back to this Julie McGuire?

Or should I scrunch the note up, toss it into the garbage, and never think of it again?

"Shawn, mate," I say to the dark corner of the room. "Tell me. It's your bass. Do you want me to give it back?"

But there's no answer. Not from the cables, or the mike stands, or even the amplifier.

Even the thing on the floor stays where it is.

I take a long breath, fold the note into a one-inch square, and slide it into my wallet.

I plug in the soldering iron, and wait for it to heat up. Once that's done, it takes less than a minute to re-connect the broken cable, and not much longer to screw the plastic panel back on.

With that done, it's time for something to eat.

On the way out of the door something catches my eye. I scoop it up off the floor. Zack's napkin, with the chords for "Day Tripper."

Right. Of course. Zack will know what to do. I'll ask him tomorrow.

5
THURSDAY

Horoscope: April 15, Aquarius:
Sharing your deepest secrets could be
especially romantic today when you unexpectedly
run into an old acquaintance. If someone has
been buying into your optimistic predictions
about the future, then you may need to face
the music when the facts are discovered.

"How about the Nowhere Men?" says Zack, when I meet him on the seafront the following morning. "I've been thinking about it all night, and I think it sounds good."

"Maybe," I say, as we jog down the long flight of steps into what was once the Municipal Air Raid Shelter, but is now the Port Jackson Aquarium. "I found something weird in the bass, yesterday."

This is our annual field trip. I should be psyched to spend a morning wandering around the spooky, dimly lit galleries. But now I have to make a decision as to how to deal with the note. Luckily, Zack ought to know the answer.

Before we even have time to glance at so much as a goldfish, we're ushered into an auditorium so we can spend our first hour being lectured by our spooky, dimly lit biology teacher, who is none other than Mr. Frost, or *Frosty* to those in the know.

"Did you fix it, though?" Zack slides into a chair near the door and dumps his backpack on the desk in front of him.

"Yeah. It's fine," I say. I throw down my backpack next to his, and watch the rest of our class file in. "But guess what?"

Frosty marches to the front of the class and tosses a pile of clipboards onto the lectern.

"I think the Nowhere Men could work as a name," says Zack. "It's Beatles-related and it's kind of surreal." He crouches behind our two backpacks like a soldier under fire. "Guess what, what?"

"Morning!" Frosty clamps his paws onto either edge of his desk as if he's about to snap it in half.

"Morning," comes the chorus of reply.

I sit up straight, but Zack sinks even lower behind his backpack.

Frosty turns to the blackboard and chalks the word, F-I-S-H. "A fish," he says, "is a gill-bearing, aquatic, vertebrate animal that doesn't have any limbs with digits."

"Zack, mate," I mumble. "Something weird happened

after you went home." I pull my exercise book out of my notebook, jot down limbs with digits, and then lean closer to Zack. "I opened up the bass. I found the loose wire, and I soldered it back together, but guess what else I found?"

"I don't know." Zack takes out his own notebook and a chewed-up pen. "The Lost City of Atlantis is actually located under Shawn's bed?" He tries to scrawl some words, but the pen just makes empty furrows in the paper. "What do you think of the Nowhere Men as a name?" He leans over to me. "You got a spare pen? This one's knackered."

"Right." Frosty pivots around to face us. "Unlike groupings such as birds or mammals, fish are not a single clade but a paraphyletic collection of taxa, including," he counts on his fingers, "hagfishes, lampreys, sharks, rays, ray-finned fish, coelacanths, and lungfish."

"This might be pretty important as well." I dig the note out of my wallet, slide it under the metal pocket-clip of my spare pen, and hand both items to Zack. "Shawn's bass was stolen."

Frosty leans on the top of an empty desk. "What was that, Toby Holland?" He flexes his elbows as if he's about to spring.

"I was just telling Zack that I'm really interested in fish," I say.

"I don't object to you talking in class, Holland," Frosty takes off his jacket, "as long as you don't mind me failing you."

"Sorry, sir," I say.

45

Frosty hangs his jacket on the back of the chair. Most of the teachers wear shirts that are tight across the stomach, but loose around the chest. Frosty's shirt is baggy round his waist, and so tight across the chest that any sudden move could probably split it.

Zack unrolls the note from the pen, fishes his John Lennon glasses out of his pocket, and slides them on. "Do these make me look interested in fish?" He looks down at the note.

"Only in lungfish," I say as I watch him read.

When he's finished he puffs up his cheeks and blows out a long breath.

"That's weird, right?" I say. "I mean, Shawn is no thief. He paid for the bass, but maybe the person he bought it off stole it. What do you think that means legally?"

Zack gives me an odd look, then he turns back to his exercise book and copies down the notes from the board. "Legally?" he says. "It means nothing. I think that if you have the bass in your possession for more than a year, it becomes your property. You've had the bass for more than a year, right?"

"Yeah," I reach over and take his glasses off his face. "About eighteen months." I put the glasses on and squint from side to side as if I can't see anything. "Do I look cool yet?"

"On the other hand," says Zack as he retrieves his glasses, "you could argue that if you discover it's stolen, then you have a kind of moral obligation to give it back."

"So I should give it back?" I say.

"No." Zack shakes his head fiercely. "It would be Shawn's decision anyway, but there's another factor." Zack throws his pen down onto the pad. "This Julie McGuire might have sold the bass and forgotten to take the note out."

"Seems a bit far-fetched," I say.

Frosty glances toward me so I duck down behind my pack and draw squiggly lines on my pad. Hopefully it looks like I'm diligently taking notes.

"It's not," says Zack. "There was a bloke who left a note like this one in his car when he sold it, and he got sued." Zack picks up the pen and puts in it his mouth. "It could also be a prank, but worse than that, it could be some kind of scam. It might have been left there deliberately."

"But look at the handwriting." I point at his mouth. "Do you mind," I say. "That's my pen you're chomping on."

Zack pulls the pen out and stares at it. "Bloody hell," he says. "Sorry."

I say, "It's obviously a girl's writing."

"Girls do scams and pranks as well." Zack hands me back my pen.

"But it's nice writing." I make a big show of wiping the pen on my sleeve. "That note was written by someone who was honest and sincere."

"Look how old it is though." Zack hands me back the note. "It's yellow around the edges." I glance toward the front of the auditorium. "Like some biology teachers. It could have been there for a decade."

"You can say that again." I take the note from Zack. I'm just about to slide it back into my wallet when the dimly lit room seems to get a little dimmer. I look up. The light is being eclipsed by Frosty leaning over my desk.

"Holland!" he snarls. "You are a vile little man. Did you know that?"

For a second I consider telling Frosty that my ex-girlfriend Katrina had called me something similar, but then I change my mind. "No, sir," I say as I shove the note into my wallet. I'm not sure this is the right answer.

Frosty holds out a hand the size of a small tennis racket. I reach over and shake it. The hand remains rigid. "The note, you noxious clown," he says. "Give me the note."

I'm about to protest that I don't know what he's talking about when he says, "The note you just put in your wallet."

"It's very private, sir." I resist the urge to take it out.

"Nevertheless," he says, "I would like to take a look at it. When I have read it I will return it to you."

I blow out a long breath and reach back into my wallet.

"You will then go straight back to school with your note," says Frosty, "plus another note that I will write."

I place the note on the desk between us.

"Then you will take both notes to the head." Frosty unfolds the note, and pushes his glasses onto his forehead to read. The crimson color of his face turns to orange, then pale pink, and finally back to deep vermillion. He grunts. "What is this?" He tosses the note back onto the desk.

"I found it in something I bought," I say, skirting

the truth. "I wanted to show it to Zack. His dad being in insurance. I thought he might know what to do."

Frosty grunts again. "Don't do it during class." He takes two clipboards from under his arm and hands one each to me and Zack. He prods the clipboard in front of me with his finger. "These are multiple-choice questions," he says. "Bear in mind that we're looking at fish." He points out toward the galleries. "Not everything out there is a fish."

We shoulder our packs, file out of the classroom, and line up in front of our first dappled, blue-green exhibit: an underwater rockscape that at first glance seems empty, and then from behind a boulder glides one of the weirdest things I've ever seen. It's a harbor seal, looking like a flying dog with no ears.

"Get a load of this fellow." Blue light ripples across Zack's face as he turns to me. "Stop worrying about the bass. Be happy. Like him." He points at the tank.

A few more glide out from behind the rocks. Are seals happy? I watch them zip up and down the tank. They seem fairly at ease with the hand the universe has dealt them, but does that make them happy?

"They might be happy," I say, "but they aren't really fish."

"Toby," says Zack. "Why do you have to split hairs. I think I'm going to go and search for a happy fish, and then study it."

"Later," I say.

"Later," he says, as he walks away, "and think about calling us the Nowhere Men."

Attached to my clipboard is a sheet with twenty questions about fish. I read though them until I get to one about the number of gills that sharks have, so I trundle off to the shark tank. Sharks are at the top of the food chain, so if there's a happy fish it's probably going to be a shark.

I follow the signs through what seems like several miles of tunnel until, almost by accident, I stumble across a group of motionless, shadowy figures with staring eyes and gaping mouths. And those are just a group of ten-year-old kids standing around watching the sharks. I join the circle, and within moments I'm totally mesmerized by the long, dark shapes gliding around the drum-shaped tank. The thing about sharks is that they never look quite the way you expect them to. They look more fishy. More real.

Or maybe it's just that I'm used to seeing sharks in films, and they look less real, which might be partly due to their being made from plasticine and cardboard. Difficult to know if they're happy, although it's probably unfair to judge by these ones, as they're probably the equivalent of sharks in prison.

After some unknowable amount of time, all but one of the ten-year-olds wander away. The kid who stays behind is tiny with floppy hair and a pair of spectacles with lenses almost as thick as the glass of the shark tank itself.

He uses these spectacles to scrutinize the information

board. In fact, he's studying it so avidly I get the impression he's looking for errors.

I need to answer the question about sharks, so I close my own gaping jaws, wander over to the board, and skim the text from over the kid's shoulder.

All I get to read is that the tank contains sand tiger sharks, nurse sharks, and a blacktip reef shark, and they all have jaws that open and close automatically. Then the kid sneers at me, shakes his head in disdain, and moves in front of me, blocking the section I was reading.

I check my front for spilled food, and my fly, but there's nothing. I have no idea why this kid has taken an instant dislike to me. I suppose he just wants to indulge his fascination with sharks in private. I'm sure one day he will have his own shark-infested swimming pool, and if anyone tries to read over his shoulder they will be going for a dip in the deep end.

There are some other kinds of fish swimming around the tank with the sharks. I can't really tell if the sharks are happy, but I think it's a fair bet that the other fish are pretty stressed out. In the realms of reincarnation, I wouldn't want to come back as a fish that shares a tank with a shark, even if the shark is a nurse shark. They look like they have long memories and bear grudges.

I wander around to the other side of the tank. Partly to see if there are any other sharks, and partly because the geeky kid is giving me the creeps and I like the idea of having about a dozen sharks between me and him.

The opposite side is uninhabited by humans with the exception of a girl who's sitting cross-legged on the floor, drawing.

As usual, my first thought is that she looks like Katrina, then I immediately bang my clipboard on my forehead because she's nothing like Katrina.

I can't account for what I do next.

Maybe it's my last hundred or so conversations with Zack about girlfriends.

Maybe it's reading about how sharks look scary but they're not really.

Maybe I actually concussed myself with the clipboard.

But anyway, I do something completely out of character for me.

I wander over to the girl, check out her picture, and say, "Sand tiger shark. Looks pretty good."

"Thanks," she says. She half-glances around at my knees, then goes on with her drawing. I study the dark hair radiating out from the crown of her head. I have no idea why she made me think of Katrina. Katrina was blonde and tall. This girl is dark-haired, and looks to be quite short, not that it's easy to tell when she's sitting on the floor.

Not my type at all.

I flip through my activity sheet until I find the question about the sand tiger shark's gills. "Carchiarias taurus," I say, more to myself than anything else.

She stops drawing, twists right around, and looks up at me. "Bloody nora!" she says, and leaps to her feet and crouches into something that looks like a kung-fu stance. "You've got a flipping nerve. I'll give you that!"

There, standing right in front of me, is the girl I bumped into yesterday.

6
THURSDAY

My whole body screams at me to run, but out of the corner of my eye I can still see the ten-year-old kid. I grit my teeth. I refuse to run away from a five-foot-tall girl in the presence of a bespectacled primary-school geek.

"You know what." I clear my throat. "You are the one who has the nerve," I say, and I think I'm going to stop right there, but the words just keep coming, and I can't stop them. "You were out of order yesterday. You saw that car try to run me down, and what do you do? You act all like Miss Goody Two-shoes." I put on a squeaky voice. "Eww. You touched me."

Her mouth narrows to a slot.

Maybe I went too far with the squeaky voice.

But, no.

She points at my chest with her very sharp-looking pencil. "I did not say any such thing, and anyway, you call that touched? You want to look up the word 'touched' in a bloody dictionary?"

I shuffle back a couple of paces, out of range of her sharp pencil, and hold my clipboard in front of my chest like a shield.

"Touched is probably in the dictionary under 'tore.'" She points her pencil up toward the street. "As in tore my arm out of its socket." She rolls her right shoulder up and down, then winces.

"I did not dislocate your shoulder." I lower my clipboard but keep it close at hand.

"You know what?" she says. "I was planning on having a nice game of golf this morning. I wasn't planning on spending a sunny day in this stinking cave." She points her pencil behind her. "Now I can't lift my arm above my shoulder. I've barely got enough movement to draw."

"Really?" I say.

"Yes. Really," she says. "I might never be able to draw properly again."

"Golf?" I say. "You really play golf?"

"You have a problem with that?" She slumps back down to the floor again and crosses her legs.

"No. No problem," I say. "I didn't realize I hit you

55

that hard." I put my clipboard behind my back. "I'm really sorry."

"You already apologized." She scoots around to face the shark tank, turning her back on me. "I'm not interested in sorry. Sorry doesn't cut it. What's done is done."

"I'm still sorry, and I really do feel bad about what happened," I say. I soften my knees and crouch at her level, but not too close. That pencil is still sharp.

"What. You're sorry you dislocated my humerus?" She glances over her shoulder at me. "Or you're sorry you made an arse of yourself."

"Both. I think. I did make an arse of myself, but I feel really bad about your shoulder." I lower myself into a sitting position. "Do you think it'll be okay in a day or two?"

"Well, you'd better hope I'm okay for your sake," she says without looking at me. "Otherwise my dad will sue the arse off you."

I lean toward her. "Hi. I'm Toby Holland." I offer her my hand. "You're probably going to need my name if you're going to sue me."

She studies my hand for a moment, then looks at my face. "Is this some lame attempt at a pick up, because if it is, Buster, you're going to have about as much chance as one of the minnows they're going to toss into that shark tank in about ten minutes."

This would be the perfect time to walk away, but somehow my legs won't work. Maybe I really did hit myself too hard with the clipboard.

"I'm not trying to pick you up." I fold my arms. "My name is Toby, not Buster, and I didn't know it was you when I commented about your picture." I pull my feet in so I'm sitting cross-legged. "If I had known it was you, I still would have come over and said sorry. And I still like your picture."

I don't know if it's my imagination, but her glare seems to soften for a moment. "Really?" she says. "You really think it's okay?"

"I really do," I say. "I wish I could draw that well."

"Nah. It's rubbish." She uses the pencil to push her hair behind her ear. "To be honest I wasn't drawing, I was mostly erasing, but there's a problem with these pencils." She waves the pencil in front of my nose. "The erasers wear down quicker than the leads, so if you're like me and you spend equal amounts of time erasing and writing, then a pencil is only useful as long as the eraser lasts, which isn't very long. I think they should make special pencils for people like me. They would be a long eraser on a very short pencil." She points to the drawing with a stubby finger. "It's supposed to be a female sand tiger shark, but I've got the anal fins totally buggered up."

"Anal fins?" I say.

"Yes," she says. "Anal fins. You have a problem with that as well?"

"I thought that was one of the things you were supposed to avoid in polite conversation," I say. "You know, politics, sex, religion, and anal fins."

Her mouth gets small.

Oops. I've gone too far again. I was just getting through to her. Me and my big mouth.

"Are you trying to be funny with me?" She scoots around to face me while still cross-legged. "I have an idea," she says. "Why don't you leave me alone and go and talk to that ten-year-old kid with the big glasses?" she says. "He looks about the right age to find the idea of anal fins humorous."

"You know what's funny?" I say. "I already tried that. I told him a joke about anal fins, and he sent me over here as he thought you might appreciate it."

She scowls at me for a long moment, then scoots back around to face the shark tank. She turns a page in her sketchbook and begins a new drawing. Without looking at me she says, "I'm going to ignore you now, but because you were nice about my picture I'm going to let you know that I'm not ignoring you out of some strategy to hide the fact that I like you." She draws a few lines, says "crap," then turns to me and says, "I'm actually ignoring you because I don't like you, I have no interest in you, we have nothing in common."

With that she tears out the page, scrunches it up, and throws it onto the tiles next to her. She turns to the next page, but it already has a drawing on it, which is of a bird. She flips through a couple more pages and then pauses on a page with a drawing of another bird.

A very familiar-looking bird.

"You know what else is funny?" I say, pointing to her book.

"Nothing is funny." She turns a few more pages until she comes to blank one. "Funny peculiar maybe. Funny-not-funny maybe. But funny ha-ha. Not a chance."

"Actually it's funny peculiar." I switch the arrangement of my legs. Sitting cross-legged on a concrete floor is harder than it looks. "Something else strange happened just before I saw you yesterday."

"Don't mind me," she says. "I'm just ignoring you."

"You know that bird you have a drawing of, three pages back," I say. "The stocky grey and white one, with the stripey chest. I saw one. It flew right past me."

She stops drawing, freezes, then looks over at me. "Is this the beginning of some kind of joke?"

"No. Straight up. Dead serious." I switch my legs again. "I saw one of those birds. Or at least something very like it."

She turns back the pages, until she comes to it. "This one?" she says. "You saw one fly right by you?"

"Yup," I say. "That's the one."

"Which means it probably flew right past me," she says. She folds up the book and stands to face me. "Sunny Jim," she says, "or Toby, whatever your name is. I don't know what planet you're from, and I don't really care, but that bird is a Peregrine Falcon." She taps her pencil on the book. "They are incredibly rare, and the last one that lived in this region was shot just after the First World War." She twirls the pencil around her fingers. "They have not been seen here since. You probably saw a pigeon or a seagull, and maybe it was carrying something that made it look striped."

"Look," I say. "I'm not an opthamologist…"

"Ornithologist," she says.

"Ornithologist," I say, "but I know what a pigeon looks like, and I know what a seagull looks like. This bird flew so close to me I could almost touch it. It was the bird in your drawing."

"Okay." She spreads her arms. "Take me to where you saw it. Show me the bird, and I will bring my guidebook to the birds of the coastal regions, and I'll prove to you that it was not a Peregrine. We can go now, if you like."

"Actually I'm on a school field trip," I say. "I can't go now, and I'm busy this evening as well."

"Okay, tomorrow," she says. "Oh, and before you ask, I'm from Brunswick. We haven't started back at school yet. I forgot that you lot have."

"Saturday at four o'clock," I say. "In front of the big statue in Memento Park."

"Four o'clock it is," she says.

"Can I ask you one more thing?" I straighten my legs, which have gone numb, so I rub them.

"Okay," she says.

"I know this is a long shot," I say, as I stand up, "but what would happen if by some freak chance the bird I saw really was a Peregrine Falcon?"

"I don't know." She hugs her sketchbook to her chest. "I hadn't even thought about that. You could laugh at me."

I shake my head. "I'm not the laughing type," I say.

"No." She leans sideways and scrutinizes me as closely as if I'm one of the exhibits. "You're not, are you." She frowns, but then something odd happens. Her frown softens. She doesn't exactly smile, but she no longer looks completely hostile. She says, "Maybe I would let you buy me a cup of tea."

There's an abrupt scrape and clatter as three women in Wellington boots enter the shark room.

She twists around to look at them, then turns back to me. "Hey look," she says, and just for a moment she actually smiles. She looks right into my eyes and smiles. "They're about to feed the sharks. You want to watch?" Then, as suddenly as she started smiling, she stops and narrows her mouth back to a slot, as if she's been caught doing something she shouldn't.

"No," I say. "I think it would make me uncomfortable. I'm feeling a little minnow-like just now."

The girls laugh as one of them pulls down a ladder from beside the tank.

"You should tell me your name," I say. "Just so when the court summons arrives I'll know who it's from."

"Michelle," she says. "Michelle Frost, if you want the whole thing."

"Michelle?" I say.

"Please," she says. "If you can find it in your heart to do one thing for me, then please do not sing my name."

"No. I had no intention of singing to you," I say. "I

just thought—" I spread my arms. "I remember your friend called you Shelly."

"Shelly. Michelle," she says. "It's an abbreviation."

"See you tomorrow at four." She glances around at the shark girls, then turns back to face me. "Toby."

"Prepare yourself for a cup of tea on Saturday." I back away from her toward the entrance, then say. "Michelle."

7
THURSDAY

The first thing I do when I get in from school is to try the bass and make sure my soldering worked. I switch on the amp, turn the volume down, and plug it in.

Fantastic.

No crackling.

No popping.

No cutting out.

With that done, I empty my pockets of the day's accumulated crap. As I do, I find the note. I stare at it for a moment, take it out, smooth it on my knee, and read it again. Am I such a bad person? Michelle obviously thinks I am, otherwise why would she have been so rude to me?

Zack is wrong. This isn't a prank or a scam. Not only was Zack wrong, but Frosty was right. I should have shown the note to Zack at some quiet moment. How could anyone look at this note and not hear a genuine pleading voice? So what if the note was written years ago. Julie McGuire, whoever she is, still deserves to get her bass back. I should call her, and I should call her right now, before I have second thoughts.

I'm not even doing this for the reward. Two hundred pounds isn't going to get me another bass as good as this one. On the other hand, maybe I could negotiate for a bigger reward. One that's adjusted for inflation.

One thing is for sure. If I don't ring I will spend the rest of my life wondering what I should have done.

I reread the number as I head downstairs with the note, but Mom is on the phone.

"Sadly, I heard it was going to cloud over for the next few days." Mom's voice drifts out of the kitchen door.

She is sitting at the table with a big smile and the phone glued to the side of her head. She glances briefly at me as I walk in, then turns her attention back to the pile of envelopes scattered in front of her.

"It's such a shame," she says into the phone. "I really thought we might get summer early this year."

An open can of coffee, a scoop, and a pack of filters surround the coffee machine. She must have been interrupted in the middle of making coffee. I'll be the good son. I take the glass container over to the tap and fill it.

"No." Mom taps a pen on the table. "I know you can't do anything right now, but I really do appreciate your help."

I take the container back to the machine and put the filter in. It doesn't fit.

"Thank you, Shirley." Mom doodles a skull and cross-bones on one of the envelopes. "You too. Bye, bye." She hits end, drops the phone onto the table, and blows out a long, ragged breath. "Bloody imbecile."

"Friend of yours?" I hold up one of the filters. "I think these are the wrong size."

She turns toward me as if I've just woken her up. "It's an experiment. I'm using the wrong size filters." She resumes studying the pile of envelopes.

"Does it work?" I say. "I mean, do you get better coffee?"

"Sorry, darling," she says without looking at me. "It's a joke. They sold me the wrong size yesterday at Preston's." She pushes the chair back. "Here. I'll do it. They work. They just need to be squashed down."

"It's okay. I've got it." I stuff the filter into its holder. "A perfect fit." I point to the envelopes. "Anything from Shawn?"

She shakes her head. "Nope." She picks up the envelope with the skull doodle. "I had a nice note from my credit card company, though."

"Really? I thought they just sent you bills," I say.

"Not at all. Listen." She pulls a page out of the envelope

and unfolds it. "Dear Emily Holland." She grins at me. "That's nice isn't it?"

"I suppose," I say.

"Dear Emily Holland, it has come to our attention that your account is now a thousand pounds over your credit limit. Please rectify this matter within five days, otherwise we may be forced to initiate a recovery action." She studies the top of the letter. "Arrived today, dated ten days ago."

"Can't you call them?" I switch on the coffee machine.

She presses her hands to her cheeks. "Oh, now why didn't I think of that?"

The coffee machine gurgles.

"Sorry." I pull two cups off the rack above the sink. "Was that who you were just talking to? It sounded like a friend." I line up the cups in front of the coffee machine. "Is it all sorted out?"

"Not completely," she says. "I got transferred to half a dozen different departments, only to be told that I had to speak to the twenty-four-hour service department, and they go home at five o'clock."

"That makes no sense at all." I get the milk out of the fridge. "Man. I would have given them some choice language." I pour the coffee and give Mom one of the cups.

"Thanks," says Mom. "As your granddad used to say, *Always be firm, fair, and friendly.*" She turns the cup handle toward her, lifts the cup, and takes a sip. "So that was my friendly act. You never know. Sometimes if you're nice to people they're nice back to you. Although on the other hand your grandfather also used to say, *no good deed goes unwasted.*"

"How come you're a thousand in the red?" I say.

"It's all my fault." She bangs the cup down. "I've been splurging like a drunken sailor." She blows out her cheeks.

"I thought we were broke," I say. "What did you spend it on?"

"Oh, you know. Rent, food, electricity," she says. "Frivolous stuff."

I lean on the counter and take a sip of my coffee. "Couldn't you ask Shawn?"

"I haven't heard from Shawn for a couple of weeks," she says. "Anyway he helped out with that monstrous electricity bill a couple of months ago. We have to leave him with something for himself. You know, being a sailor he of all people should be allowed to splurge like a drunken one now and again."

"There has to be another way we can raise some cash," I say.

"Of course. I could sell my jewels," says Mom. "I never wear the tiara anymore."

"You have a tiara?" I say.

"Sorry," says Mom. "Bad attempt at humor. Listen, how much do you think all of Shawn's music stuff is worth?"

"But you can't sell Shawn's stuff," I say. "He'd be devastated."

"Sweetheart," she says. "When he helped out with the electric bill he actually said if you get into any more money troubles have Toby sell my music stuff. You should be able to get a grand if you're lucky."

I shake my head. "The bass is the most valuable thing," I say. "It's worth maybe three-fifty. The amp, maybe two hundred. The keyboard, a hundred. Then there's all of the mics, cables, and stands. That's maybe another hundred. That makes seven-fifty if we get what we ask for."

"Enjoy it while you can, Tobe," she says. "If it comes to a choice of living on the streets and selling Shawn's equipment, then I'm afraid the equipment will have to go."

"But Mom," I say. "We have a gig on Monday at the old Jubilee Cinema. It could be the first of many."

"Keep your hair on, Tobe," she says. "Hopefully it won't come to that." She pats my shoulder.

"I thought you could come," I say. "I could put you on the guest list, and you wouldn't have to pay to go in."

"I'll have to see if I can get the time off," she says. "I have a lot of applications for real jobs out there. One of them is bound to work out, and I only need one."

"We shouldn't have come here," I say. "I mean, to Port Jackson. It was probably a mistake, wasn't it?"

"I don't know," says Mom. "It seemed like the right thing at the time. How would you feel if we went back to London?"

"Could we wait a couple of months?" I say.

"Why don't we give it till school ends for the summer," she says. "That's a month. If I can't get a job that actually pays enough to live on within the next month, then I think it's a fair enough that we go back."

"Will it be easier in London?" I say.

"There's a job waiting for me whenever I want it back," says Mom. "Listen, I'm going to watch the news. You go and finish your homework."

8
THURSDAY

"Could I make a phone call?" I say.

"Of course." She gathers up her coffee and the envelopes, then heads for the door.

"It's to Brunswick," I say. "Is that long distance?"

"It is," says Mom, "but it's after six so you're okay. Do you have the number?" she says.

"No. I was just going to dial some random digits," I say.

She ignores my comment and says, "Do you have the code for Brunswick?"

I shake my head.

"01375." She almost smiles. "Don't talk too long," she says, "or I really will take your bass away."

Mom leaves and I push the door closed. I take out the note and examine it.

What am I going to say?

Why am I even doing this?

Maybe I'll just hang up if she answers. I think I just want to know if Julie McGuire is real. I want to know that should it become necessary, I could give her the bass back, although I'm not sure how I'm going to find that out from a phone call.

I dial the code, then the number.

The phone makes a weird beeping sound, and a robot woman says, "The number you have dialed is not available. Please check your number and dial again."

I key in the number again, but get the same message. I examine the note to see if there's another hidden number, or if I've read it wrong, but it's fairly clear.

I open the kitchen door and call to Mom, "The code for Brunswick is 01375, right?"

"01375," comes the reply.

I try yet again, and still get the robo-woman.

I turn off the light, and head out into the hall.

"Did you get ahold of them?" says Mom from the living room.

"No," I say. "I just keep getting the wrong-number message."

"What's the number?" she says.

I push open the door to the living room. She's lying on the sofa with a pair of glasses propped on her nose. She holds out a hand for the note, but I just read it out to her. I don't want her to know what's in the rest of the note. "553554."

"Is that it?" She sits up.

"Were you expecting more?" I say.

"Actually yes," she says. "You only have six digits. They added a three to the start of all the Brunswick numbers a few years ago."

"A few years ago?" I say.

"You know, I'm not sure. More than five years ago I think," she says. "If you don't mind me asking, how on earth did you come by an out-of-date number for Brunswick?"

"It's just an old friend of Shawn's," I say.

She pushes up her glasses. "Does this person have a name?"

"Mom!" I say. "Do I have to tell you everything?"

"Toby," says Mom. "I don't think you know this, but Shawn had some iffy friends. Not good people to be mixed up with."

"What do you mean by iffy friends?" I say.

"Just not a good crowd," she says.

"I'll give it one more try," I say. "It's an old number. I'm probably not going to get through to them anyway."

I go back to the kitchen. I dial the Brunswick code, the three, and then the number. I'm so convinced that I'm going to get robo-woman again that I almost put the phone down. But it rings. It rings four times, and finally someone answers.

Nobody speaks. I wait for one, two, three heartbeats. Maybe the line went dead. "Hello?" I say.

"Good evening, good sir." A man's voice. Maybe about Frosty's age, and with an accent. It sounds to me like an English person putting on an American accent. Or maybe it's an American impersonating an English accent.

"Oh, hello," I say again. I was so ready for no answer that I haven't thought how I was going to approach this. "I'm sorry to bother you—"

"It's no sweat," he says quickly. "What can I do for you? Hey, I recognize your accent. Are you calling from London? I love London. I'm hoping to get down there before too long. Yeah. Buckingham Palace, Paddington Station, Kensington Gardens. Cool."

"Oh, no. I live in Port Jackson, actually." I sense this is not going to be easy, but I think about Mom, and the firm, fair, and friendly thing. "Look, this is probably a long shot—"

He interrupts again. "Port Jackson. Yeah, Port Jackson is a cool place. I've had some fine times there in the past. Maybe some fine times still to come if you know what I mean."

I have no idea how to respond to this so I just say, "I'm trying to trace someone by the name of Julie McGuire. I was wondering if she still lived there."

He doesn't respond for a while. Maybe he's hung up.

I'm just about to put the phone down again when I hear laughter in the background, presumably from a TV.

Then it's his voice again. "Julie McGuire?" he says. "You know, now that you mention her name, I do get the feeling I know her. Maybe if you could give me some clue as to what this is about it might jog my memory?"

"My brother had the number," I say. I'm not sure how much information I should give out over the phone to a stranger, but he sounds trustworthy, and maybe that firm, fair, and friendly rule works. It would be fair to trust him unless I have a really good reason not to, and if I'm friendly I might find what I need to know. "He's in the navy, and we were sorting out his things, and we found this number."

I pause to see if this jogs his memory, but he doesn't say anything.

"You see," I say, "he had something that belongs to Julie, and we'd like to give it back."

"What kind of thing?" he says.

Okay. Maybe it's risky to give out so much detail, but he's really the only lead I have to Julie, so I suppose I'm going to have to chance it. "A bass guitar. An electric bass," I say.

There's a pause. I hear more laughter in the background, and then a sound that is obviously clapping, but it actually makes me think of rain.

"An electric bass?" he says, and pauses again.

Maybe he doesn't know what an electric bass is.

I start to say, "It's like an electric guitar—"

"Oh, no," he says. "I know what an electric bass is."

More clapping in the background.

"Yeah," he says. "You would want to give that back. Those things can be pretty valuable. Hey, don't tell me. It's not a Fender is it?"

Is this bloke beginning to get a little too curious, or is it just me being paranoid? Be fair and friendly. "You know," I say, "does any of this ring a bell? I mean if you don't know Julie McGuire—"

"Whereabouts are you in Port Jackson?" he says.

"Listen," I say. "I need to go. I'm sorry I bothered you."

"Wait a minute," he says. "I'm pretty certain I can help you. By the way, I used to live just above Memento Park. Brackett Street. You know it?"

"Sure." I really don't want to be rude to this guy, but I think I have to. To be honest, he sounds drunk. Maybe I should try him again when he's sober. "I know it well. Listen. Does Julie still live there? I can't really talk for long. My mom's worried about the phone bill."

"No problem, my friend," he says. "I get the picture in full color, and in 3-D. No problem. So you're near Memento Park?"

"I have to go," I say.

"You know," he says. "I bet you live in one of the season streets. You're not in Summer Street are you? I used to have a really good friend in Summer Street."

"No," I say.

"What's that?" he says. "No you don't live in Summer Street, or no you don't live in the seasons streets?"

"I'm going to hang up," I say. "My mom is standing behind me. She wants to use the phone."

"Oh, I understand," he says. "I completely understand. Here, why don't you leave your name and number, and I'll call you back."

I take the phone away from my hand. Just before I put my hand over the earpiece, I hear his voice but not what he says. I put the handset back on its cradle.

I take a long breath with my eyes shut. How could I be so stupid? I might as well have told him everything. He probably has caller ID. He knows my number. I stare at the phone a while longer. If he calls back I want to pick up right away. But he doesn't call back. Maybe if he's drunk he won't remember the call. I back away from the phone as if it's an unpredictable dog. I get halfway up the stairs. I turn again. Still it doesn't ring.

I was wrong. Zack was right. Trying to give back the bass is just a waste of time.

Finally, I get back to my room and take out the note again. It could easily be fake. It could even have been written by the bloke I was just speaking to. The thought makes my stomach turn.

I take out my copy of *Fahrenheit 451* and turn to the title page.

Written in neat blue ink are the words: Katrina Morgan. I hold the note next to Katrina's handwriting.

Totally different.

9
SEPTEMBER LAST YEAR

It was the final evening of the summer holidays last year and I was standing on Katrina's doorstep. I had my back to the door and the whole of Port Jackson in front of me.

I breathed in the cool air, and strode across the front lawn. Her parents preferred me to use the path, but it wound around the flower beds a little too much for my liking, and I was feeling in a direct kind of mood that evening.

As I stepped gingerly between the stalks of lilies and chrysanthemums, I pondered some of the things Katrina had told me. Apparently being sex-obsessed was only the tip of the iceberg. I was also rude, mean, selfish, and dishonest. In short, I was a bad, bad person, and that is why I had been dumped.

Having just been dumped, I didn't really feel in the mood to sit in my room and do homework, so I headed toward the downtown area, which was almost ninety degrees to my route home.

I took Denmark Street, which goes all the way into the shopping district. The only problem with Denmark Street was that it went past school. I'd been to school enough times already today, and I had enough bad memories to keep me going for one evening, so I took a detour that looked like it went in the right direction. Ombard Street, the sign said, although it looked like some of it might have been broken off. It was a side road I'd never been on before. According to my sense of direction, Ombard Street should have allowed me to bypass the school by a couple of blocks, then get back onto Denmark Street. Naturally this was not my night, and Ombard Street turned sharply and immediately came to a dead end. But at the dead end, with all its lights spilling out onto the dark street, was a music shop.

I had a bass. It was my brother's, and I'd been playing it for a year or so while he was away. I'd always thought I should have my own instrument. Maybe that was a sign of my selfishness, that I was happy to play someone else's guitar rather than provide my own. I crossed the narrow street and went inside.

The door pinged once as I opened it, and again as I closed it. The room I'd stepped into looked as if a tipper truck full of old, battered, and unwanted musical equipment had been emptied into it. It was crammed floor to ceiling with instruments I recognized, including saxophones, trumpets, trombones, accordions, and violins, but there were a number of instruments I'd never seen before. Dangling from the ceiling was something that looked like a combination of a saxophone and a trumpet. Right next to it was a violin with a triangular body, and standing next to the door was a trombone with piano keys.

At first I thought the place was empty, but then an echoing voice said "Good evening." Even with the echo, I could tell that the voice had a faint foreign accent of some kind.

Once I got used to the dim light, I could see that there was actually a pathway between the piles of instruments on the floor. I made my way down this path toward where the voice had come from.

Next to the counter was what appeared to be a seven-foot-tall saxophone with a pair of trouser legs attached to it. With the other weird instruments, I wasn't surprised to see a sax with legs but then the legs moved back, revealing that they were not actually part of the instrument, but belonged to a man with a face the color of rosewood and shoulder-length dreads. Clutched in his hands were a number of rods and plates, presumably from the sax.

"May I help you?" he asked. I could hear the accent more strongly now. Maybe it was a little French, but not really from any place I could put my finger on. He put his head back into the gigantic bell of the sax.

I did a quick survey of everything that was hanging from the ceiling. Drums, cymbals, bits of oboes, cellos, banjos, and bongos, but no guitars or basses I could see. Maybe it was one of those shops that only catered to the kind of musicians who wore thick glasses and beards without mustaches.

"Do you have any electric guitars or basses?" I said.

"Upstairs," came the reply. Without taking his head out of the sax he pointed to the back corner of the showroom with a screwdriver. I stepped carefully in the direction of the screwdriver. Hidden in the shadows was a narrow flight of steps with a handwritten sign saying guitars and basses.

"Thanks," I said, and climbed the stairs.

The second floor was even more amazing than the first. I almost felt like I ought to genuflect. Or maybe it was more a museum than a church, because three of the four walls were jammed to bursting point with electric guitars and basses, all different colors and shapes, and all of them either old or ancient.

The instruments dangling from the first wall were totally in keeping with the downstairs. All crazy shapes and colors. I didn't recognize a single one.

Not so the second wall. This one was taken up by Japanese copies of famous American guitars. These were all well made, and good to play. It was the third wall that got my attention though. These were all the original American guitars and basses, made by Gibson, Fender, Rickenbacker, and Gretsch. The Cadillacs of the guitar universe.

The fourth wall was a window that looked out onto Ombard Street.

The first thing I did was start counting the instruments, but I got sidetracked at the twentieth one. It was a p-bass, the same as Shawn's, but this one was really battered. Most of the lacquer was gone, leaving the bare wood of the body. The price tag said ninety-nine, ninety-nine. I could afford that. I could get a part-time job and it wouldn't take me too long to save up. I pulled the bass off the wall, propped it on my knee, and plucked a few notes. Funnily enough, for a bass that looked like a piece of driftwood, it felt really good to play. I moved up and down the fret board. It was perfectly in tune. I turned around, sat on the stool, and plugged the instrument into the amplifier. I placed my fingers on the fret board and plucked three notes. I could feel the sound in my mouth. It made me swallow. Before I could play another note, a series of footsteps hammered up the little staircase. A face appeared in the doorway before the notes even stopped ringing off the walls. The older gent from downstairs.

"Stop," he pleaded, with his palms out. "Stop!"

I froze with my hands hovering just above the strings. Was it dangerous? Was it toxic? Would my hair fall out now that I'd touched it?

The gent crossed the room in about three steps. He slid the guitar off my lap. I was as rigid as a shop dummy.

"It is a 1962 Fender Precision bass," gasped the gent as he placed it back on the wall, hooking its little loop of guitar string over the hook.

"But it's only ninety-nine pounds," I said. "I could buy it."

"Nine thousand," muttered the gent, "nine hundred and ninety-nine pounds. I'm selling it for a collector friend of mine. It's not just the most valuable instrument you have ever touched." He prodded himself in the chest with his thumb. "It's the most valuable instrument I have ever touched."

"I'm sorry," I said.

"It's okay," said the gent. He reached past me, unhooked another p-bass from the wall, and handed it to me.

He said, "Give it a whirl."

This time I folded my fingers around the neck and body as if it was a priceless vase. As if the slightest knock would shatter it. Then I sat down on the stool with it.

The gent shuffled around behind me, plugged one end of a lead into an amp, then plugged the other end into the bass.

I played a quick blues line. I felt I was supposed to comment so I said, "Sounds nice."

He gave me a not-quite-a-grin, and said, "Put it through its paces." Then he turned his back on me and clumped back downstairs.

Once he was gone I relaxed and began playing a bass line I'd heard on the radio a couple of days earlier. I ran through it a couple of times. I was just about to start a third verse when a voice next to me made me jump.

"Brilliant," said the voice. "That's 'Nowhere Man,' right?"

I was so shocked that I almost dropped the guitar. The owner of the voice was a kid from school. I'd seen him a few times, but I didn't know him. "Yup. 'Nowhere Man,'" I said. "You have a good ear."

"Thanks," he said. "My dad played my first Beatles record when I was a baby," he said, "and I haven't stopped listening to them since." He reached his hand over to me. "I'm Zack, by the way. If you don't mind me asking, are you in a band?"

I twisted around in my seat so I could reach over the bass and shake his hand. "Not at the moment," I said.

He sat down on top of the amp. "I've been trying to put together a band for a while," he said. "And I want to play mostly Beatles stuff."

"Good idea," I said. "The songs are great. Everybody likes them."

He spread his hands. "I don't have a bass player yet. I mean, would you be interested?"

To be honest, my first thought was to say no, but then I thought back about what Katrina said about me not having any friends. I think I just wanted to prove her wrong. I nodded. "We could give it a go."

"I think it's going to be amazing." Zack sprung up, and selected a telecaster from the wall. "This is what I have," he said, then pointed at the p-bass on my knees. "You have your own axe, right?"

I was going to say yeah, sure, but Katrina came back to me again, with all that stuff about me being devious, so I said, "I have my brother's p-bass. He's in the Navy so he doesn't use it."

"Do you think he's going to want it back?" said Zack.

"It's not so much that," I said. "It's more like I don't feel right about using his stuff while he's away. I was trying to find one of my own."

"Let's do 'Nowhere Man.'" Zack sat down opposite me, and plugged his guitar into the same amp. I counted us in. We played a couple of verses with me playing bass and Zack playing chords, and then he jumped in with the guitar solo. I'd never listened to it that carefully before, but Zack was playing it note-for-note exactly as it was on the record, and I realized right away that it was a difficult solo, and that Zack was a pretty good musician.

"That's amazing," I said. "You make it look so easy."

"I mostly play along to records," he said. "It's the first time I've ever played it with someone else." He pointed to my bass. "Is your brother's bass as good as that?"

"I think it might be better, actually," I said. "You know, I was wondering. Are all p-basses worth like ten thousand pounds?"

"No." He reached over and peered at the swinging tag on the one I was playing, which I hadn't noticed. "This one is only four hundred. I think the older they are the more valuable they are."

"My brother's p-bass is old," I said.

"Could be worth something," said Zack. "Are you thinking of selling it?"

"No way," I said. "It's not mine to sell. I was just thinking if it was valuable it ought to be insured."

"Ask Harry," said Zack. "He can tell you how much it's worth in an instant."

"Is that Harry downstairs?" I said.

"Yeah. Harry Haller," said Zack. "It's his shop. He's a great guy."

"My ears are burning."

We both turned to face Harry Haller, who was once again at the top of the stairs.

"That sounded very nice," he said, "but I'm afraid I have to kick you out. My wife has dinner on the table, and she does not care for cold food when it is supposed to be hot."

"Thank you for letting me play, Mr. Haller." I handed him back the bass. "Sorry about the other bass."

"You can call me Harry." He hooked it back in its slot and turned to me. "You're welcome to play any instrument in the store, but please ask me first before you take down any of the old Gibsons and Fenders."

"My brother has a p-bass," I said. "I think it's pretty old. I was wondering how much it was worth. I mean, I should get it insured if it's valuable."

He grinned at me. "What is your name, my friend?"

"Toby."

"I could take a quick look, Toby, and give you a ball-park figure," he said. "I charge twenty pounds to do a full evaluation, and if it's an old precision bass, then you should do that. You will need to get it properly insured, and an insurance company will honor my evaluation."

"But the most it could be worth is about ten thousand," I said.

Harry Haller laughed, and pointed to the one I'd played earlier. "This one is just the most valuable instrument I have played. A couple of months ago a precision bass was sold in New York for a hundred thousand dollars."

"Yikes," said Zack.

"And the prices are still going up," said Harry. "The p-bass you were playing is ten years old. It's just a second-hand bass, not worth as much as a new one. The bass I rescued from you is about thirty years old. You know how much that one is worth. The p-bass that sold for a hundred thousand dollars was nearly sixty years old."

"Wow."

"Does your brother's bass have a solid case?" said Harry.

"No, just a gig bag. A soft case," I said.

"Follow me." Harry led us downstairs. He rooted around behind the counter and produced something that looked like a black coffin. "Here. Take this," he said. "It's a precision case. It's old. It's solid, and it's very heavy, but it will protect your bass in all but the worst accidents, and you look pretty strong."

"I don't have any money on me," I said.

"Take it," said Harry. "Bring it back if you buy a better one. It's just taking up space here."

"Thanks," I said.

"What did I tell you?" said Zack. "A really decent bloke."

10
FRIDAY

Horoscope: April 16, Aquarius:

You are feeling especially attractive today.
The voices that whisper softly in your ear are
the ones you will hear loudest. Relax and tune in
to your body's natural rhythms.

Up in Shawn's room we plow straight through every Beatles song we know.

"Ticket to Ride" goes off without a hitch. I stay focused from the opening riff to the final chord, but "Can't Buy Me Love" is a different matter. At some point around the second chorus, my mind wanders and I find myself on a sunny evening leaning against the Memento Park statue. Michelle appears in the distance. My heart quickens and I push myself away from the statue, dust off my clothes, and push my hair behind my ears. But as Michelle gets closer, I can tell she's just a little too tall to be Michelle. She passes a few yards away from me and I wonder how I ever thought she was Michelle. When the song ends I'm jerked back to the reality of Shawn's room.

The next three songs, "Tell Me Why," "Get Back," and "I Should Have Known Better," also go smoothly; then we get to "Revolution." Once again, the song begins with me on full alert, and then I'm back at the statue. Once again, I spy Michelle in the distance, but this time as she approaches, she's heavier than the real Michelle.

I almost get through "Eight Days a Week" before I'm back at the statue again. In this scenario, I get there late and Michelle is waiting for me wearing a pink dress. She's facing away from me and she looks like she's gained a little weight since the Aquarium.

"Hi," I say. "Michelle!"

Slowly she turns. It's not Michelle at all but Jasper Hamilton-Sinclair in makeup.

This spooks me so much that when we play the last two songs, "Day Tripper" and "Lady Madonna," my mind doesn't wander even once. Maybe that's the secret. Terror focuses the mind.

Zack doesn't seem to notice any of my lapses of concentration, and when we reach the end of "Lady Madonna" we both slump back onto Shawn's bed.

"We have a set," says Zack. "We actually have a set. Except I think we need to switch 'Day Tripper' with 'Lady Madonna.'"

"You think we should play more?" I say.

"No. I think we're good. I don't think we should try to overdo it." Zack drags his jacket onto his knees. "More to the point, I've got a treat for us. Special from Harry." He pulls a paper bag out of his pocket and holds it up proudly. "New strings for both of us."

"Man. That's about twenty quid's worth of strings," I say.

Zack pulls two packs from the paper bag. One set of guitar strings for him, and one set of bass strings for me. He tosses the bass strings over to me.

Zack props his guitar between his knees and begins slacking off his old low-E. The guitar makes a deep twanging sound. He takes out the new string, which is coiled into an "O." He unravels it and with well-practiced moves, he fits one end to the bridge, draws the other end up the neck to the machine head, then lets out a long sigh.

"Listen," he says. "Please don't flip out, but I told my old man about the bass."

"Why on earth did you do that?" I have the first new string out of the pack, but instead of uncoiling it out of its "O" shape I spin it around my first finger.

"Well, you know, he deals with insurance claims." Zack already has his second string fastened to the machine head, and is starting on the third. His guitar looks ten years younger already. "He knows the legal ins and outs, and I don't want you thinking you've got to give the bass back." Zack lets go of the string he's working on, and it flicks back with a twang.

"So?" I use the pointed tip of the new string to clean my thumbnail. "What did he say?"

"No. You don't have to give it back." Zack threads the fourth string into its slot. "It would help if Shawn had a receipt, but it's not essential. I was right about the time limit. There's a statute of limitations. If the bass has been in your possession for more than a certain amount of time, then it's technically yours." He studies me like I'm some weird cloud formation on the horizon. "But he told me something else."

"There's always something else, right?" I say.

Zack's new strings gleams in contrast to the old ones, which have almost turned black.

"He thinks that Shawn probably did steal it," says Zack.

I watch Zack in silence as he coils the old, corroded strings around his fist, then I let out a long breath.

"Aren't you going to say anything?" says Zack, as he pulls the fifth string out of its wallet. "Are you really pissed off at me?"

I reel in the bass string like a fishing line and shake my head. "Mom knew," I say, "and she didn't tell me. She said Shawn had some iffy friends." I think about Shawn bringing all the stuff in late at night. He was always coming home with something, and it was always late at night. Why do I have to be the last to know?

"From what my old man told me that's a generous assessment," says Zack. "I mean, I love Shawn. Everyone does. He's a great guy, but he was a criminal." Zack's guitar is now fully rigged with shimmering new strings.

"But how come people liked him if he was a thief?" I say. "That doesn't make sense."

"He was Robin Hood." Zack tosses the first of the old strings across the room into the wastebasket. "A lot of thieves steal from people who are actually quite close to them. Shawn wasn't like that. He stole from businesses." Zack throws the second and third strings at the wastebasket, but they miss and bounce into the corner. "It was actually what made him popular. Not only did everyone love to see him sticking it to rich people, he virtually gave away everything he stole for ridiculously low prices. If you wanted something, you asked Shawn." Zack retrieves the strings from the corner, and places them into the bin. "And he still made money. That was why he ended up as a tar." A drop of blood appears on the tip of Zack's index finger. One of the strings must have cut him. He places his finger in his mouth and sucks it. "The police were on to Shawn. Things began to get uncomfortable. What better place than 5,000 miles away from the people who want to see you in the slammer?"

"You're telling me he joined the Navy to get away from the police?" I say.

"In a nutshell," says Zack.

"So none of this stuff is really his?" I use the new string to point to all the band equipment scattered in loose piles around the room.

Zack shakes his head. "Probably not."

"Do you think he stole the bass from Harry's?" I say.

"Nah," says Zack. "He wouldn't steal from Harry. He didn't steal from people he cared about."

"I think he did steal from ordinary people," I say. I rest the bass on the floor, and put the strings on top of it. "I don't think he was a Robin Hood at all."

This news wipes the smile off Zack's face. "What makes you say that?"

I walk over to Shawn's nightstand. I open the top drawer. I fumble around until I find what I'm looking for, then toss the wallets onto Zack's lap. "I thought he had a wallet collection," I say. "I thought it was something he had a thing for. I was half right. He did like collecting wallets. Other people's wallets."

Zack picks up the wallets one by one. Now it's his turn to look astonished. He shakes his head. "Well, bugger me backward," he says under his breath. I open the second drawer down. Inside are more wallets, some cell phones, keys, dozens of keys on rings and tags, and watches. There are about twenty or more watches. They're mostly cheap digital ones, but one or two are fancier-looking.

"I had no idea," says Zack. "I had no clue to the real Shawn."

"Yeah, well that makes two of us," I say as I hold up one of the watches.

Meanwhile, one particular wallet seems to have caught Zack's attention. It's a slender brown leather one. "I lost my wallet a couple of years ago. I thought I'd put it down and lost it. Only had a few quid in it, but I really liked it. I think this is it."

I put the watches back in the drawer. "Then there's this," I say. I take out the note again. "The bass belonged to a girl," I say. "I mean look at the little hearts over the I's. Grown women don't do that."

Zack takes the note, but doesn't read it. "Whatever happened has happened, and the deed has been done. You can't undo what's been done."

He returns the note to me. I fold it up again and put it back in my wallet.

"You're not going to go to Brunswick and just give the bass back, are you?" Zack rests his guitar across his knees and strums the riff from "Ticket to Ride."

I shake my head.

"I'm glad to hear it." He stops playing and makes some adjustments to the tuning. "It's a heartrending note, but you can't do it. It just won't work." He starts playing "Ticket to Ride" again. "I feel really bad for this girl, Julie, but I'd feel worse for you and Shawn if you actually went through with it. You can't un-steal something that was stolen, especially if it was stolen two or three years ago."

"I don't think there is a Julie McGuire." I pick up the bass, and try to get myself into tune with Zack. "Or maybe there is, but she didn't write the note. I think it's some kind of scam."

"Wow," says Zack. "You changed your tune. What brought that on?"

I draw in a long breath. "I rang the number."

"Oh man! Toby," says Zack. "What did she say?"

"It was a guy," I say. "A really weird guy."

Zack begins "Ticket to Ride" yet again, and this time I follow along with the bass part.

"It's sounding really good," says Zack. "How much did you tell this bloke?"

"Virtually nothing," I say.

"Thank God for that," says Zack. "Just don't call him again."

I shake my head. "I didn't need to tell him anything," I say. "All I did was ask him if Julie McGuire was there and right away he knew exactly why I was calling. It almost felt like he could see me through the phone."

"Don't stress about it, mate." Zack pats me on the shoulder. "Just let sleeping dogs lie."

11
SATURDAY

Horoscope: April 17, Aquarius:

You will wake up feeling especially confident today. Your decisiveness and self—assurance will lift the spirits of everyone around you.

By the time Saturday rolls around I think I've probably imagined every conceivable scenario involving Michelle, Memento Park, and myself. Some of them I've imagined so many time it's like watching endless reruns on TV.

I play through some of them as I'm down on the bedroom floor doing my push-ups.

The leading contender is the one where I show up and Michelle doesn't. End of story.

By this time, another old favorite is the one where she shows up, but she's brought along her friend from the other day. Not the end of the story; just the start of one that's not terribly interesting.

I've only once envisioned the scenario where Michelle shows up, and she's holding hands with Jasper Hamilton-Sinclair. But once was more than enough.

I've even been imagining the scenario in my sleep, like the dream I had on Friday night when I showed up, and Michelle showed up, but it turned out I wasn't wearing any trousers.

I head down to the kitchen, put the kettle on for tea, and find myself lying on the floor while I wait for it to boil.

Not to pray, even though that might be an avenue worth exploring, but doing extra push-ups in a last-minute attempt to turn myself into somebody more impressive before I head off to the park.

Then, as I'm struggling to push myself up off the floor for about the fifteenth time, I imagine a brand-new scenario.

In this one, it's me who doesn't show up.

It's simple. It's brilliant. And I have no idea why didn't I think of it before.

I roll over and sit with my legs crossed as a Zen-like calmness washes over me.

This infuses my entire being until I get to my feet to finish making tea, and bang my head on the kitchen table.

I watch some old cartoons on TV.

I write an essay about sharks; quite a good one actually. I get within a couple of chapters of the end of *Fahrenheit 451*.

I practice few songs. I strum through "Lady Madonna,"

but when I reach the line where it says Sunday morning creeps like a nun, I have another realization.

My Saturday morning is more like a nun trying to roll a boulder up a hill.

This not-turning-up business is harder than it looks. You can't just make the decision not to show up on the spur of the moment. It has to be planned well in advance. I should have planned a fun alternative, like a day trip to the beach, or London, or New Zealand.

The upshot is that an hour later I somehow find myself waiting under the statue. What makes it worse is that it's only three o'clock and we planned to meet at four. I look up and scan the flat grey sky for the falcon.

I really couldn't have done a worse job of planning this. It might be a little foolhardy to rely on a somewhat-unfriendly girl to show up.

But to rely on wildlife to show up?

That's totally daft.

One more thing hits me along with this realization.

It's a raindrop, and it smacks me in the middle of my forehead.

A second one hits me in the eye.

I do another quick survey of the sky, this time in search of blue. There is none. It's the color of Shawn's destroyer from one end to the other.

This is no quick squall. Once the rain gets into its stride, it's going to keep raining for hours and, naturally

I'm dressed for a sunny afternoon. I need to find somewhere dry for the next hour, and I know just the place.

Five minutes later I wander into Harry Haller's.

12
SATURDAY

It's been six months since my last visit to Harry Haller's. I never did bring in Shawn's bass to have him value it, but nothing much has changed about the place. For all I know, it could be the same collection of instruments dangling from the ceiling. Even Harry looks the same, the only difference being that last time he was fixing a saxophone, and this time he's fixing what I think is a balalaika.

"Can I help you?" He looks down the neck of the balalaika and gives me his almost-smile. Probably doesn't recognize me, which is not surprising. All the business of organizing our gig has been done between him and Zack. I wasn't involved.

"I was going to look at your basses." I point to the staircase.

"Help yourself," he says.

As I make my way up to the guitar room, I realize that I can do more than just stay dry here while I wait to go back to the park. I'm not planning to give Julie McGuire back her bass, but if for some reason I had to, and she made good on the offer of the reward, then this might not be a bad time to see what two hundred could buy me.

A quick glance at the Fender and Gibson wall is all I need to know that I'm not even close to being able to buy another Fender Precision. Even the wall of Japanese copies has only a couple of instruments within my price range. I lift one off the wall. A bright red p-bass with a maple neck. I only play three notes before I hang it back up.

I head to the wall of mystery guitars. There's a Burns Bison, a Watkins Rapier, and a Vox Teardrop all within my price range, but what really catches my eye is a Strad Bass, exactly like the one Paul McCartney played back in the early days. I take it off the wall. At two-fifty, it's a little out of my league, but it's playable.

I sit down and start thrumming my way through my repertoire of Beatles bass lines, beginning, of course, with "Nowhere Man."

I've only been playing for a couple of minutes when

I hear a loud drumming. I glance over at the window. It looks like someone is spraying a fire hose at the glass.

The rain has started with a vengeance. Maybe it'll slacken off before I have to go back to the park.

I'm just about to start playing again when I hear footsteps on the stairs. I stop and freeze. I really don't want Harry Haller whisking an instrument out of my hands again. But it isn't Harry. It's a lean man in a pork pie hat and sunglasses. Water drips off the brim of his hat and onto the damp-looking shoulders of his leather jacket.

The hat I can understand. It's good protection in the rain, but the sunglasses? Even with the lights on it's so dark in here that I can barely read the price tags.

"Good evening, good sir," says the man, and raises his hat an inch or so off his head. "That sounded very nice. Don't let me stop you playing. Everybody loves the Beatles." He wanders over to the wall of Fenders and Gibsons. "Way cool. Way cool."

I go back to strumming, but I don't feel quite so much like playing with this bloke wandering around. Then I start thinking about the gig. If I feel this self-conscious in front of one person, then how am I going to be able to play in front of a whole audience on Monday?

I watch him as he wanders. He seems to be interested in p-basses. He examines two or three of them, and then there's another set of footsteps on the stairs. This time it is Harry Haller, and he really does come and lift the Strad Bass out of my hands. "That's an instrument to hang on somebody's wall," he says, with a slightly warmer version of his almost-smile. "You'll ruin your technique if you play something that bad." He hangs it back up, selects the Watkins Rapier, and hands that one to me.

"Thanks," I say. "I was just thinking that Paul McCartney always looked cool playing a strad bass in the old photos."

"I can't say for certain," says Harry, "but he probably just posed with the Strad Bass, whereas this one," he points to the one in my hands, "is one of the best basses in the shop." Harry stands back, rubs his hands together, and actually grins at me. "As good as any Fender, and only one hundred-eighty quid."

"One hundred-eighty?" I say. I immediately think that I could buy this with the reward from Shawn's bass. That's if I do give it back. I probably won't, I suppose.

"One hundred and eighty," repeats Harry, turning to look at Pork-pie.

But Pork-pie is staring at me. "He-e-e-y," he says. He has a p-bass in his hands, which he is holding left-handed, even though it's a right-handed instrument. In other words, upside down. "I like your accent," he says. "Where are from?"

"London," I say. I feel hesitant about telling him this. I don't really like talking to people wearing sunglasses, especially when I don't know who they are. It feels like they're trying to hide something.

I go back to noodling on the bass.

"London is the place to be," says Pork-pie. "You've got to be in the heart if you want to make it beat."

"Excuse me, my friend," Harry says to Pork-pie. "What exactly are you looking for?"

"I know exactly what I'm looking for." Pork-pie tips the p-bass from one side to the other.

I watch his fingers as he pulls a string. It makes a flat, dead, clunk.

"A 1960s precision bass," he says.

I glance up at Pork-pie's face. He's not looking at Harry, the bass, or at his fingers. He's staring right at me.

"Sunburst body," he says. "Rosewood neck. Very cool. Very slick."

I try to take my eyes away from Pork-pie's, but I can't seem to move. Hair prickles on the back of my neck.

"That's an '80s p-bass you have there," says Harry. "It's pretty decent. Why don't you give it a whirl?"

Finally, Pork-pie looks away from me. I slump down as if I'd been held up by strings. He looks over at Harry.

"Me? I'm a pure artist, good sir." Pork-pie flips the bass over onto its back. "I can only play when the stars are aligned and the spirit moves across the water. I can only play when the muse is in the heavenly house." He flips the bass forward again, but it's still the wrong way round to play. "And the only instrument pure enough to receive my ministrations is a p-bass from the 1960s."

Could Shawn's bass be a 1960s one?

Harry lets out a long breath. "A '60s p-bass will set you

back at least five grand." He smiles at Pork-pie, and raises one eyebrow. "You have an expensive muse."

Could Shawn's bass be worth five thousand pounds?

"My talent is a gift from the gods," says Pork-pie. "No dollar spent would be wasted, and worth every cent." He hands the p-bass to Harry, and then directs his sunglasses at me again.

Once again, I can't move.

"You sure you don't have one?" he says, and I'm not sure if he's talking to me or to Harry. "Maybe somebody brought in one to sell to you. Or maybe you just sold one."

Finally, Pork-pie looks away again.

"Maybe I could contact the buyer and make an offer," he says.

"No. I'm afraid not," says Harry. "I wish I did have one to sell you. I had a natural wood p-bass a few months back, and that one went for nine thousand." Harry spreads his arms, then slaps them against his thighs.

"Natural wood?" says Pork-pie. "That means it wasn't painted. Right?"

"Correct," says Harry.

"Could it have been a p-bass with the paint peeled off?" says Pork-pie.

"There are natural basses that are *natural* because they have been stripped at some point," says Harry. He grins as if he's in some pain. "This particular one was a *natural* natural."

"There are two other places you could look in Port

Jackson," Harry adds. "Steve's Sounds and Merrywether Music."

"I checked those guys out," says Pork-pie. He heads over to the stairs. Harry follows him.

Pork-pie says, "Gave them the once over, but no joy, no luck. Beautiful people. Very friendly." He shifts his hat to one side. "Can I leave you a contact number?"

"Of course," says Harry.

"Please call me if anybody brings one in," says Pork-pie. "Be cool. Let me know. Hey. Even if they don't want to sell. Maybe just getting it valued or fixed or something. Let me know. I'll make an offer." He hands Harry a card with something scrawled on it.

Harry looks at the card as they make their way down the steep staircase. "You're based in Brunswick? You should look closer to home. You'll have far more luck."

As the voices fade away downstairs I suddenly realize that I have to leave right now to get to the park.

I hang the bass back on the wall, jog down to the first floor, and make my way to the entrance. Just as I push the door open to leave, Harry looks up and says, "You play in the band with Zack don't you?"

"Yes," I say. "I'm really excited about Monday." I step backward and let the door close. "I was just running through the set." I point upstairs.

"Sounded very tight. Your timing is good. That's very important for the bass." Harry runs his fingers along the neck of the balalaika. "I remember you telling me that you had an old precision bass."

"Yes!" I come back into the store. "I was going to mention it to that bloke who was just in here, but I thought it might not be the right thing."

"Your instincts were correct," says Harry. "That gentleman was ... " He twirls his finger around. "How do you say ... ?"

"Artsy-fartsy?" I suggest.

"Full of shit," says Harry. He breaks into a full grin and gives a short, coughing laugh. "I would not recommend you do any business with him." He puts down the balalaika and offers me a card, presumably the one Porkpie just gave him. "If you want to contact him, please leave me out of it."

"It's okay." I shake my head. "Are you saying he's some kind of criminal?"

Harry shrugs, and turns his attention back to his balalaika. "Just avoid him at all costs."

"Thanks for the advice," I say. "Listen. I have to go. I'm meeting someone, and I'm already late."

"Don't leave her standing in the rain," he says. "That would not be good manners."

This time I push the door open and actually leave.

13
SATURDAY

I stand in Harry's doorway for a moment. The rain is hammering on the pavement and seems to have set in for the day. I wish I had a pork pie hat now myself. There's a black Honda Civic parked across the street. It's a quiet street and even though there are plenty of empty spaces, the car is double-parked.

For really no good reason, I wonder if the car belongs to Pork-pie, and at precisely the moment the thought enters my head, the door swings open and out he steps.

He waves to me. "How are you, good sir?" he says, as if we've been good friends for a long time. He grins at me, crouches low, and pretends to draw a pair of six guns from his pocket as if he's a Western gunslinger. "Pop-pop-pop," he says, then twirls his pretend guns and re-holsters them. "I was going to offer you a lift." He pulls his hat lower, turns up the collar of his jacket, and saunters across the street toward me.

Once again, I find it difficult to move, or even think while he's staring at me, but as he gets closer I notice that he's actually shorter than me, and puny-looking as well. Upstairs in Harry's I was sitting, and he looked much taller. I should try harder not to be intimidated by him.

"I'm okay, thanks." I point upward. "It's only water."

"Very cool," he says. He reaches the pavement and stops a few feet in front of me. "Only water." He seems to be oblivious to the rain, which is hammering onto his hat and running over the brim in little rivulets. "I like it." He folds his arms, exposing a blue Hawaiian shirt under his jacket, which looks really out of place on a day like this. "I would like to apologize on behalf of this region for the less-than-delightful weather."

"Thanks," I say, folding my own arms and retreating a few inches back into Harry's doorway.

"And as a token of my regret," he says, "I would like to offer you a lift to wherever you need to get to. Free of charge and gratis." With this, he takes a couple of steps forward, effectively blocking Harry's doorway and my escape route.

I shake my head, which sends out my own mini-shower of raindrops. "I'm fine," I say. "I really don't mind the rain."

"I was thinking, you know, musician to musician." Pork-pie shimmies his narrow hips from side to side, sliding his shoes on the slick pavement. "We could take in some rare grooves. I have a kick-ass hi-fi in my car." He points back across the street to the Civic, as if I hadn't just seen him get out of it.

"It's very kind of you," I say, and I get a mental image of him back inside Harry's with the bass upside down. Maybe taunting him might get rid of him. "I didn't know you were a musician."

Pork-pie stiffens, and his mouth narrows into a slot, but only for a moment. "Oh man, I'm a key player. I toured the clubs. I even tasted the big time, but I bit off more than I could chew. I spat it out and roamed to smaller pastures where the grass was greener and more to my liking. I could tell you stories."

"What instrument do you play?" I ask him.

"What's my poison?" Harry begins to shimmy again. "I'm into a little of everything. A little bass, a little guitar, a little percussion, a little keyboards. If it can make a sound I can draw sweet music out of it."

I glance at my watch. If I'm going to go, I need to leave right now. "It's been a treat chatting with you," I say. I step forward at forty-five degrees, intending to squeeze past him, but just as I get out of the doorway something jerks me back. For a second, I think that my jacket has caught on a nail or something. I turn to unsnag it, and catch sight of a knobbly, pink hand fastened to my shoulder.

He might be small and puny looking, but his grip is ten times stronger than Jasper Hamilton-Sinclair's. I try to twist around, but it's futile. With a sinking feeling, I cannot move an inch forward or back.

"Come, good sir," he says, with a broad smile. "Don't be a fool. It makes no sense to walk in this weather."

His other hand fastens on to my forearm and, without me doing anything, my feet slide across the wet pavement toward the curb.

"Whoa! Wait," I say. "What are you? Police or something?"

"Something," he says, and then he's stopped by a ping.

Harry's door opens a few inches, and Harry pokes his head out. "Excuse me, mister," he says to Pork-pie. He holds up Pork-pie's card. "I have something that might be of interest to you."

We both stop and turn. Pork-pie's fingernails are now digging into my shoulder.

"If you have a moment," says Harry.

Pork-pie's grip slackens a little.

"If not, I can ring you later," says Harry.

Pork-pie glances at me, then back at Harry. "Don't move a muscle," he says. "I don't want you walking in the rain."

"I'm not going anywhere," I say.

Pork-pie loosens his grip and follows Harry back into the shop. As soon as the door pings shut, I take off.

At the end of Ombard Street I pause and look back, but nobody is following me, and the Civic is still double-parked. I climb Sprague Street, and cross the railway foot-bridge. From the embankment I can see Harry's shop. No black Honda is parked outside. I jog the rest of the way to the park.

14
SATURDAY

My heart is still pounding by the time I reach the park. The big statue of the World War II pilot looms through the mist, which makes me feel a little better. It's foggy enough that Pork-pie will have a hard time finding me.

On the other hand, there's nobody standing underneath the statue. In fact, there's nobody in the entire park apart from some die-hard soccer players.

I'm just about to turn and jog home when I catch sight of a lone figure under a big pink umbrella. She's heading away from the statue and toward Portland Road.

It has to be her. Nobody else would have any reason

whatsoever to be in the park on an afternoon like this. I shift direction, and sprint toward the umbrella.

"Michelle!" I wave my arms up and down a couple of times just in case she can't see me in the fog, but then I stop. I'm not sure how low an opinion she has of me just at the moment, but I don't think it's going to be improved by seeing me charging down a hill flapping my arms at her.

She pivots toward me, like a pink mushroom, and I can just about make out her face in the dark shadows under the umbrella.

"I'm so sorry." I stop running to catch my breath, and walk the last twenty yards toward her.

"Toby," she says. "You might want to think about arranging to meet people somewhere warm and dry in future."

"Yeah," I say. "I really am sorry. We should have met in the café."

"I was thinking more along the lines of the South of France," she says.

"Yeah, the South of France would be nice." Now I wish I'd brought my own rain slicker with the hood. My hair is soaked, and little icy rivulets are running down my forehead. "Did you see the falcon yet?"

"Thank you for asking. Yes, I am wet and I have been waiting for about ten minutes." She tilts the umbrella upward, giving me a better look at her face. Why do scary and beautiful always go together? "And no, I didn't see any falcon."

"There really is a cafeteria," I say. A tendril of wet hair tumbles into my eye, so I brush it back. "It's a couple of minutes walk, but we could have a warm drink and dry off."

"You're a sly one." She twirls the umbrella.

"I don't understand," I say.

"The deal was," she says, pushing her hair behind her ears, "you show me the falcon, and then I'll consent to letting you buy me a cup of tea."

"I was just thinking you might want to dry off," I say. "That's all."

"Don't sweat it. It's only water," she says. "Mostly."

"So is sweat," I say. "Mostly."

She peers up at the sky from under the umbrella. "Do you want to join me under here? If you get any wetter I may have to fight the urge to start feeding you sardines out of a bucket."

"As a matter of fact," I say, "I quite like sardines out of a bucket."

She shifts over to one side of the metal rod to make room for me.

"Thanks." I duck my head down under the rim of the umbrella and slide in next to her, making sure that no part of my shoulder or arm touches her. The last girl I was this close to was Katrina, and I can't help noticing how different Michelle smells. Katrina smelled of soap, but Michelle smells more like chai tea. Is this going to spoil my future enjoyment of chai? To be fair, my experience with Katrina hasn't really affected my appreciation of soap either way.

"You know, I was seriously considering not showing up," she says as she pulls her wind-blown hair away from her face.

"Do you want to hear something funny?" I say.

"As long as it's funny-peculiar," she says.

"I wasn't going to show up either."

"Now that would be funny," she says. "It would be like the old tree-falling-in-the-forest thingy."

"I'm not sure I follow you," I say.

"You know the saying," she says. "If a tree falls in the forest and nobody sees it, then does it really fall?"

"Okay," I say.

"So if two people arrange to go out," she says, "and neither of them show up, then would anybody ever know?"

"Next time you might want to go out with someone smarter than me," I say. "Maybe Sir Isaac Newton, or Pythagoras." I shove my hands into my pockets and listen to the rain rattling on the top of the umbrella. "I didn't think we were 'going out.'"

"We're not going out." She twirls the umbrella. "I was just theorizing about a hypothetical going out. Why weren't you going to show up?"

"Put it this way," I say. "If it had been warm and sunny, I wouldn't have come."

"Really?" she says. "You mean you would have felt guilty about leaving me standing in the rain?"

"Why weren't you going to show up?" I say.

"I'll tell you another time," she says.

"Really?" I say. "There's going to be another time?" I point to the hill just beyond the soccer field. "I think we should go to the Overlook. I think we'll get a better view. We'll be more likely to see the falcon. That is if you're up for a walk."

"Okay." She holds the umbrella pole in front of my nose. "Would you mind doing the honors?" she says. "It's difficult for me to hold it so high up. I have a mild shoulder injury from where some lunatic tried to rugby tackle me."

"Sure." I haul my hand out of my pocket and take hold of the handle. "The guy sounds like a real creep."

"I think he meant well," she says. "But then I suppose they said that about Atilla the Hun. So, you're a Londoner, right?"

"Right." I take a few steps across the grass, making a straight line to the Overlook, but the damp floods into my sneakers, so I guide us back to the path. "The short version is that my parents got divorced." We walk around the edge of the soccer field. "Then my mom's mom, who lived here, got sick." There's a corner kick and a lot of action and shouting around the blue goal. Things do not look good for the blue team, and my heart goes out to them. "So my mom moved here with me and my brother, and we all lived in my grandmother's house, which is where we still are."

"Sounds crowded," she says.

"No," I say. A gray shape flashes overhead. I glance out from under the umbrella, but it's only a pair of pigeons.

"It's just me and my mom now. My grandmother died, and my brother joined the Navy."

"Sorry about your grandma," she says.

"It was a couple of years ago," I say. "I mean she was pretty old. She was eighty-five, and she smoked forty cigarettes a day for about seventy of her eighty-five years."

"Eighty-five?" says Michelle. "My grandma's only forty-nine."

"Wow. That's pretty young," I say. "My mom is forty-eight. That's amazing that my mom is as old as your grandma."

Michelle makes no comment, and when I look at her, she seems to be very focused on the soccer game. Then, as we pass the end of the field and reach the bottom of the hill, something pulls my arm away from my side. At first, I can't quite believe this is happening, but then I look down, and it's true. The girl who wasn't interested in me, didn't have anything in common with me, and didn't even like me has wrapped her hand around the inside of my elbow.

Once we're in among the trees, they muffle the whoops and shouts of the soccer game. Walking close to Michelle, with her holding onto my arm, I get a mix of feelings. A few minutes ago I would have almost been relieved if she hadn't shown up. Now I really hope the falcon shows itself, because I would quite like to get to know her a little better.

"How often do you see your dad?" Michelle's voice is startling in the quietness. Her words echo off the tree trunks.

"Hardly ever," I say. "Actually, I haven't seen him since we left London."

"Wow." She shakes her head. "I have this other friend who's never seen her dad since the divorce. She wouldn't talk about what happened, but I think the dad did something really bad. I mean really bad."

"Oh, no," I say. "No way. My dad didn't do anything really bad. At least not to any of us."

"You're exposing me to the elements." She takes her hand away from my elbow to adjust the umbrella, but then puts it back again. "I wasn't implying your dad was evil or something. I have this special talent. If there's a wrong thing to say, I'll go right ahead and say it."

"Don't take this the wrong way," I say, "but I think I noticed that about you." A dark shape glides through the trees ahead of us, at about eye level. I freeze, mid-stride, and wait. The bird comes nearer, then turns. It's not a falcon.

I turn to Michelle, and she's looking at me.

"Rook," she says. She must have recognized it in a fraction of a second.

"My opinion exactly," I say. "Well spotted."

She squints at me through one eye as if she can read my mind.

"By the way," I say, "don't go thinking you're the only one who has a special talent for saying the wrong thing. I think I have that too."

"I bet you don't have it as bad as I do." Now she takes

her hand out of her armpit and shoves it deep into her pocket.

"I bet I do," I tell her.

It goes quiet again, and I realize that there's no more rattling on the top of the umbrella. I say, "I think it's stopped raining," and the moment the words are out of my mouth I regret it. The umbrella was the one thing keeping us close together.

Michelle lowers the umbrella. "Oh yeah," she says. "It's even brightening up a little. Look." She shakes the water off the umbrella, folds it up, and points it at the brow of the hill where the trees end. "Shadows. The sun must be coming out."

I follow the umbrella and it's true; they're kind of pale, but there are shadows under the trees at the edge of the woods.

There's a good arm's length between us now as we walk the rest of the way to the Overlook, but the feeling of closeness I have is still there. It's still there when we reach the top and the trees end, and a yell drifts up to us from the soccer game. Probably a goal. I lead her over to the parapet. It's still misty down below, but we can just about see the yellow soccer players sprinting back to the center spot. The blue players, who are more difficult to see in the mist, all seem to have a foot-dragging kind of jog. Standing over all of them is the pilot statue, the top of which is just about at our eye level now. The pilot's heroically furrowed brow, which is now beginning to have a little shadow underneath it as the sun brightens, makes him seem deeply concerned with the outcome of the game.

I shuffle toward the wall so I'm leaning alongside her. She reaches up and tucks her hair behind her ear without looking at me. I gaze at her ear, and the tip of her nose, and her mouth. I say, "Even the team that's winning looks fed up." That's what I say, but what I think is that she might even be prettier than Katrina, and with that thought, the feeling of closeness begins to fade. I want it to start raining again so she'll hold on to my arm. I want to find a higher vantage point in the park, but there isn't one.

Finally, I want her to turn toward me, and if she does, I will kiss her.

But she doesn't turn toward me. I wish I knew what she really thought of me. Without a doubt, she's one of the rudest people I've ever met, and yet she came here to meet me. She came here in the pouring rain. She offered to share her umbrella with me. She wrapped her hand around my arm and, in spite of about a dozen opportunities, she hasn't gone home.

On the other hand, maybe she's just sticking with me to see the falcon.

"Who's winning?" she says, looking at the game.

"Yellow," I say. "I think."

"You're right," she says. "They look pretty crestfallen for a winning side." Her feet scrape on the gravel as she swivels toward me.

Is this my opportunity? Her mouth is open, and her already huge eyes get even wider.

"Whoa! Look! Toby!"

No, this is not my opportunity to kiss her.

"Above the blue goal!" She jumps about a foot off the ground, grabs me by the shoulders, and rotates me away from her so I can see. "I knew it," she says. "I knew we'd see that bloody bird. I just knew it."

I don't need to follow her pointed finger; my eyes lock onto the cross-shaped bird gliding above the soccer game. It flaps its wings a couple of times as it heads in our direction. It climbs and accelerates like no other living thing I have ever seen.

"Oh, Toby," she whispers.

Moments later its black-and-white striped underside flashes right over our heads, then it spreads its wings to land right back on top of the statue. I don't know whether to be grateful to the falcon for appearing and proving me right, or to be pissed off at it for ruining my romantic moment. Either way, I can't stop staring. It is so like being in church, I even take my hands out of my pockets and clasp them in front of my crotch.

"It's a female," hisses Michelle.

"Can you tell by the anal fins?" I say.

Michelle squints at me again. "Females are brownish in color," she says, "and bigger. "Males are grey."

I think she's about to explain that birds don't have anal

fins, but now it's my turn to point over her shoulder. "Like that?"

She spins around, and we both stare in silence at the approaching male falcon.

It hurtles toward the statue, then, at the last second, it spreads its wings, settles on the shoulder of the statue, andturns to face in the same direction as the female, who is a few feet above him on the pilot's cap.

"Bloody heck!" Michelle props the umbrella against the wall, places her hands on the top of it, then leaps up so she's standing on it. "Why do I always forget to bring the camera?" She wipes her palms on her jeans, the back pockets of which are at my eye level, then wobbles unsteadily.

Added to that, the top of the wall looks slippery after all the rain, and it's a long drop down to the soccer field.

Without even thinking I reach out to steady her, and then stop myself. Her opinion of me has probably been improved by the falcons showing up, but not quite to the point where I can grab her anywhere near her bum.

Then I realize what Shawn would do.

What Zack would do.

What any bloke would do.

I clamber up next to her. "In all fairness," I say, as I try to resist the temptation to look down, "I think this qualifies me for two cups of tea."

"Yeah." Michelle nods her head. "I thought you might." She folds her arms and looks toward me, as cool as if the ground in front of her is level, rather than a three-story drop. "Where do you want to go?"

"I know just the place," I say. "It's a little run-down, but the tea's not bad."

15
SATURDAY

"I don't think this place looks too shabby," says Michelle. "Could use a lick of paint, but I've seen worse."

"Thanks," I say as I unlock our front door. "Big of you." I push it open and let her walk in first.

She turns to me halfway through the door. "You don't have any dangerous pets, do you?" she says. "You know, dogs, cats, hamsters, crocodiles?"

"We had a crocodile, but it got depressed and we had to take him to the vet," I say as I follow her into the hall.

"A depressed crocodile?" She wipes her feet on the mat, shuffles off her coat, and hands it to me.

"We're hoping he'll snap out of it," I say, as I put the wet coats on a hanger.

She gives me her one-eyed squint.

"Tea first." I rub my hands together. "Then I'll give you the grand tour." I lead her into the kitchen, pull out the chair that Shawn used to sit in, and then head over to the sink to fill the kettle.

There are some letters on the table. I was planning on putting them away later, but as I run the tap I hear papers being shuffled.

I turn around to see Michelle holding the envelopes in front of her. "I'm sorry," she says. She shakes her head with her eyes closed. "I didn't mean to look. I just wanted to clear a space on the table."

"It's okay." I put the lid on the kettle and plug it in. "There's probably nothing personal there."

"You're going to think I'm so nosey." She lifts a sheet of lined notepaper out of the stack of letters. "I saw this. You've got a friend in Brunswick."

"No, I haven't," I say as I get the cups out. "I don't know anybody who lives in Brunswick." I throw tea bags into the cups. "Apart from you, that is."

"I'm confused." She taps the letters on the table and gives me the same look she gave me when I told her about the crocodile, except this time it's a little colder. "This is a Brunswick number."

I walk over to the table and stand behind her so I can see what she's looking at.

Written on a lined sheet of paper, which looks like it's torn from the pad that Mom keeps next to the phone, is:

Toby. Rupert called earlier. Can you call him back?
It's urgent. 01375 3554553. If poss could you call
after 6.—Mom.

I draw in a long, slow breath. Thoughts swirl around inside my head like leaves, and then slowly they drift together.

It is a Brunswick number. It's the number from the note I found in the bass. Rupert must be name of the prat on the phone.

"Rupert's not exactly a friend," I say, but then having said that, I'm not exactly sure what he is. "I'm actually in a band." I spread my hands, then slap them back against my legs. "He's, sort of, to do with that."

"Oh, wow. A marching band?" She pulls a silly grin. "I can't resist a man in uniform."

"Come on. You know what I mean," I say. "The other kind of band. Like the Beatles."

"I think I've heard of them," she says. "What do you play?"

"In fact, we're exactly like the Beatles," I say. I pause between each word, studying her face for some kind of disapproval, but her silly grin softens into a smile. It's the first time I've really seen her smile.

"We do Beatles cover versions," I say. "I play the bass."

Then I remember what she said about "Michelle" in

the Aquarium. "But, don't worry," I say. "We don't do 'Michelle,' so you won't have to hear me sing it."

"I actually love hearing Paul McCartney sing 'Michelle.'" She looks down at her feet. "It just makes me really sad." She looks back at me and bites her lip. "I didn't want to go all weepy on you back in the Aquarium."

"We don't do it, anyway," I say. "It's actually pretty difficult to play."

"But if you're the bassist, then you are the Paul of the band," she says, then she swivels around to face me. "Do you do 'Blackbird'?"

"No. But we could," I say. The kettle clicks off. I fill the cups, then go over to the fridge. "Milk?"

"Thanks," she says.

"Apart from playing the bass, I don't think I have much in common with Paul." I put a cup in front of her.

"Cheers." She picks up the cup. "Contrary to what you'd think," she says, "'Blackbird' is actually my favorite Beatles song."

"We have a gig next Monday," I say. "Listen. If you promise to come we'll do 'Blackbird.'"

She folds her lower lip over her teeth and nods. "I'll come," she says. "I'll probably have to bring Sierra. Where is it?" she licks her lips. "You don't have to do 'Blackbird' though. It seems a bit last minute if you have everything worked out."

"It's at the old Jubilee," I say. "You know it?"

"I think so," she says. "So what does Rupert play?"

"Rupert?" I say. "Rupert's not part of the band." I'm not sure I can go into detail about Rupert just now so I gesture toward the kitchen door with my teacup. "Hey. Come with me. I'll show you the gaff."

Holding my cup steady, I lead her up the stairs to the first-floor landing. "This is where it all happens." I push open the first door, and right away I wish I'd done some tidying. I let her go in first again. "This used to be my brother's room," I say, "but he's in the Navy now, so we use it for band practice."

"Whoa," she says as she stumbles on a cable and spills some tea. "Is this where you keep the depressed crocodile?"

"Take the weight off your feet." I point to the bed.

She perches right on the edge, as if she thinks I'm going to pull the bed out from underneath her.

I kneel down next to her and reach under the bed.

"Is that where you keep the depressed crocodile?" she says.

"Exactly." With quick moves, I drag out the p-bass. "This is it." I stand up and show it off. Not much light spills in through the bedroom window, but the little that does makes all the chrome and lacquer sparkle, sending tiny reflections scuttling across the ceiling.

"Wow," she says. "It's really pretty. It's easily as impressive as a depressed crocodile."

"Fender," I say. "The best."

"I bet it cost a bunch, right?" she says, then covers her

mouth. "Sorry. That was a bit of an obnoxious question. I told you I was nosey."

"It's my brother's," I say. "He bought it. He's not here, so I use it."

"It's nice of him to let you," she says. "I wish I had a brother like that."

"Do you have any brothers and sisters?" I say. I think that's the kind of question you're supposed to ask at times like this.

"Only child," she says. "As my mom says, *Accidents don't happen twice.*"

"Accidents?" I say. "That's not very nice."

"She always laughs and hugs me when she says it." Michelle slurps her tea. "But it makes me wonder sometimes."

I'm not sure what to say to this. "So." I sit on the bed next to her, and lay the bass flat on my knees. "A couple of nights ago I opened up the insides to do a repair." I pull out my wallet and take out the note. "I found this inside." I hand the note to her.

She tries to unfold the note one-handed while she's still holding her tea.

"Here. Give me that." I take the cup from her and place it on top of the amplifier. She unfolds the note and reads it. As she does, her eyebrows knit closer and closer together.

She looks up. "Let me get this straight," she says. "Your brother bought the bass, but you found this note inside it."

I nod.

"But what does this mean?" she says.

"To be honest, I don't know a lot more than you do," I say. "It might mean exactly what it says, namely that a girl called Julie is the rightful owner of this bass. On the other hand, it might be a mistake. She might have sold it and forgotten to remove the note."

"Did you try ringing this number?" she says. "Wait. You must have done. Isn't this is the same number as the one on the note from your mum?"

"Right," I say. "When I phoned, I spoke to some bloke." I study her for a moment. Maybe I'm drawing her too deeply into this. "He never told me his name. I suppose, based on the note on the kitchen table, his name must have been Rupert." I hardly know her, and everything I know about Rupert is pure conjecture. I don't want to have to tell her a lot of my theories and then have to retract them.

"And he knew all about the bass." She retrieves her cup, sips her tea, then wipes her mouth with the side of her finger. "Or maybe he didn't have a clue what you were talking about."

I choose my words carefully. "He wasn't a lot of help," I say. "If I was to make the best possible guess, I would say that Julie is no longer at that number."

"But you have the address." She takes another sip of her tea, but this time she doesn't wipe her mouth. "Like I told you. I know Mariner Street. It's not far from me."

"Wait." I stare at her lips, which are now shiny from

the tea, then I shake my head so I can concentrate on what we're actually talking about. "Let me catch up with you. Are you saying that you think I should give back the bass?"

Now it's her turn to give me a puzzled look. "Why wouldn't you?" she says. "It sounds like this poor girl really needs the bass back."

"What if I can't find her?" I finish my tea and put the cup on the floor. "What if she's moved?"

"Well…" She finishes her tea. "Maybe the people who live there now will know where she went." Once again she draws her index finger across her lips, then she slots her finger through the handle and lets the cup dangle. "If they don't then maybe you could put an ad in the paper." She places the cup on the floor, then slides it next to mine. The cups connect with a little ping.

"Unless she's dropped off the face of the earth, someone will know where she is." Michelle sits back up, turns slightly so she's facing me, and smiles with her mouth closed. "I know where Mariner Street is. You can walk from the bus station. It's about ten minutes. If you like I could go there with you." She leans forward with her elbows on her knees, and gives me a sideways look. "When it comes to knocking on the doors of strangers you might have more luck if you're with a girl."

"No," I say quickly, or rather I croak because my mouth is dry, then cough. Rupert could be living at 48B Mariner Street, and I don't want Michelle to have to deal with him. "I would rather you didn't do anything right away."

"But you've got to give it back eventually." She points to the bass, then shrugs. "You can buy another one with the reward, then you'll be able to play it with a clear conscience." Once she's said this she stares at me as if I've asked her a difficult question.

I want to tell her that I haven't had a guilty conscience about the bass, but instead I find myself leaning forward. I close my eyes and a moment later, with the bass lying between us, I brush my lips against hers. She takes my upper lip between hers, and plants a line of kisses from one corner of my mouth to the other.

I feel off balance, poised on the edge of the bed. I slide my hand up the back of her arm, and stroke her hair.

She kisses me one more time, pulls away an inch or two, then nestles her nose into my neck. "I have to go," she says in a soft voice. She brushes her hair behind her ears, then stands up.

"I'm sorry." I stand up, and put the bass on the bed. "That was totally out of order."

"No. Really," she says. "It's not that." She bends down, retrieves the teacups, and hands them to me. "It was nice."

I take the cups from her.

She brushes her hair back again and says, "I really do have to go."

"I can walk you home," I say. "It's starting to get dark."

"I think Port Jackson's pretty safe," she says. "Brunswick? Maybe not so much."

"I didn't mean because it was dangerous." I lead her

over to the door with a teacup in each hand. We make our way back down the stairs. "I don't think I'd be a lot of help if it was dangerous. I'd just like to walk with you."

"Don't get me wrong. I'd like you to walk me home," she says, as reaches the bottom of the stairs. "It's just my dad. I'm staying here with him at his house." She takes her coat off the hook, and shoves an arm into a sleeve. "You know how told you my grandma was the same age as your mum?"

"Yeah," I say. I want to help her on with her coat, but I still have a teacup in each hand.

"Well, my mum had me when she was sixteen." She buttons up her coat, and fixes me with a stare.

Maybe she's looking for a reaction.

"That's how old I am now," she says. "Mum thinks that having me messed up her life, and she's terrified I'll do the same thing."

"I'm not…" I say, waving the teacups around.

"I know you're a real gent," she says, "but mum thinks all men are the same. So I'm not supposed to be out cavorting with boyfriends." She reaches up and pulls the ends of her hair out from under her coat collar. "My dad's this total macho man." She shakes her head, splaying her hair across her shoulders. "He's into extreme sports. You know. He does that thing where you get chased by bulls in Spain. Then he climbs mountains, and goes scuba diving with sharks." She gathers her hair as if she's about make a ponytail, then lets it fall on her back. "But then he's terrified of my mom. Yeah. Figure that one out."

I open the door for her. She shuffles outside and turns back to face me. "So, basically, I'd be up shit creek if he saw us while he was walking home from work or something."

She grabs me round the back of the neck, pulls my head down to her level, and gives me a firm kiss just to the side of my mouth. The kiss is not exactly what I would call tender. In fact, it's close to the force of a headbutt. Nevertheless, a kiss is still a kiss.

She releases me from the head lock, steps back, and looks me up and down. "That's why I had second thoughts about showing up at the park."

"Now how do you feel?" I say. "Are you sorry you did?"

"What are you doing tomorrow?" she says.

"I haven't made any plans," I say. "Why? Do you want to go to the park again? Maybe we could look for some penguins."

"Why don't we go to Brunswick?" she says, and then looks at me as if it's me who's just asked her a difficult question.

In actual fact, it's me who doesn't know the answer. A trip to Brunswick would mean spending the whole day with her, but if I give the bass back tomorrow I'm not going to have anything to play on Monday night.

As if she can read my mind she says, "Don't bring the bass. It'll just be research."

I give a short laugh of relief. "Great," I say. "Fantastic."

"I'll meet you at the bus station," she says, half-turning away from me. "How does ten o'clock sound?"

"Perfect."

With that, she pirouettes and marches down to the end of driveway. She turns, gives me a final wave at the corner, and then she's gone.

I stand there for a moment, still with a teacup in each hand. After a minute I go back in and shut the door. Right away I spot her umbrella. My first thought is to run after her. Then I think that perhaps we ended on a good note. Maybe I should let sleeping dogs lie for now. The umbrella has a little tag with an address on Summer Street.

It's only a couple of streets away, but I can give it back tomorrow.

16
SATURDAY

Still holding the two cups, I head back into the kitchen. I could use more tea so I put the kettle on again.

While I wait for it to boil I sit back on Shawn's old chair, the same chair that Michelle was sitting in half an hour ago.

I pick up the pile of envelopes with the message from Rupert on the top.

I scratch my chin.

Who is he?

It's a good question.

More to the point, why did he phone?

Did he remember something about Julie McGuire?

I sift through the other letters. There are four or five offers for credit cards, and one slim letter from the Navy.

If Rupert did remember something then I suppose I should ring him back. On the other hand, I think I would rather find her without this bloke's help if it's at all possible.

I turn off the kettle, fix my tea, then head back to the table.

The first thing that catches my eye is the letter from the Navy. All thoughts about Rupert vanish and an ice cube forms in my chest. As far as I know they've never sent us anything.

Letters from Shawn are usually fat and addressed by hand. This one looks more official.

I hope it's not one of those letters they send to tell you something awful has happened.

I tap it on the table, then glance over at the kettle. I could steam it open, although if the letter really does contain what I'm dreading it might contain, then steaming it open would probably make things worse. If it does contain the dreaded news, then I should phone Mom.

With that, I know what I have to do. I take the letter out to the hall and dial Mom's number at work. I get transferred and put on hold, then finally she picks up.

"Good evening, caller," she says. "This is Emily Holland. Which of our services can we help you with today?"

"Hi, Mom," I say. "It's me. Toby."

It sounds like there's a party going on in the background, except with no music, and nobody laughing. Actually it doesn't really sound like a party at all, just a lot of people talking at the same time.

"You've got me at a bad moment, Toby," says Mom in a fierce whisper.

"I'm sorry," I say.

"Call back in twenty minutes on the other line," she says.

"Mom! Wait," I say. "There's a letter from the Navy."

"That's lovely, caller," she says in a breezy voice. "Is there anything else I can help you with?"

"Mom!" I say. "I think it might be very important."

I listen to the chattering again and a noise that sounds like a man yelling. I hope I never have to work at a place like this.

She takes in a long breath, and I know she is thinking exactly the same thing as me. "Alright. Open it, but please be quick."

Cradling the phone under my chin, I tear open the envelope, fold out the single sheet of paper, and skim it.

"Is he okay?" Mom's voice breaks into my concentration. "Whatever it is. Please tell me."

"He's okay," I say. "He's alive."

"Thank God for that," she says, and blows out a long breath. "But what? They didn't just write to tell us he's okay."

I start to speak, but my mouth is too dry so I swallow and try again. "He's in the Glasshouse," I say. "It says here that he stole something from another rating."

"The bloody fool," she says. "The bloody, bloody fool."

"But at least he's okay," I say.

"Great, he's okay for now," says Mom, "but how long's he going to be okay in that place?"

"I don't know," I say to fill up the emptiness.

"We're going to have to go back to London, Toby," she says, "so we can be near him. We have to do what we can to help him."

"I know," I say.

"Are you going to be all right with that?" she says.

"When were you thinking of leaving?" I say.

"When's your concert?" she says.

"Monday."

"I get paid on Tuesday," she says. "Let's go on Wednesday. Let me get back to work. We'll talk more when I get home."

After I hang up, I flatten out the letter and have another go at reading it. I get the general idea, but I can't focus on more than a few lines before my mind wanders and I have to go back to the start again. It's half an hour until Zack comes over, but I can't just sit here. I could practice my bass lines before he arrives.

All of a sudden I feel very tired. It seems like hours ago that Michelle was here, even though she only left about ten minutes ago.

I take another look at the note from Rupert.

Great.

Now that he has my number, he's probably going to call every day.

One good thing about leaving Port Jackson is that he won't have our London number.

I look at the phone and imagine it ringing in the empty house, day after day.

There's something that bothers me even more about the note, but the more I try to think about it the sleepier I get.

I make my way up to Shawn's room, even though he'll probably never see it again now. I stand in the doorway for a moment and take it all in. I'm going to miss a lot of places, but this is the one I'm going to miss most.

I take out the bass, put the strap over my shoulder, and give it a quick tune-up. New strings go out of tune fast. I more or less stumble across the room to the bed and flop down. I start trying to figure out the chords to "Blackbird," but I still feel tired. I let myself fall backward onto the quilt, and stare up at the cracked ceiling. I rest my fingertips on the strings, but I don't seem to have the strength to pluck them.

17
SATURDAY

I don't go to sleep, but instead drift somewhere between being awake and dreaming, and in this state one of my last memories of Shawn comes flooding back to me.

There's a loud rap on my bedroom door. It's dark. The middle of the night.

"Who's there?" I say, forcing my voice to go deep, although even like this I don't think I sound particularly intimidating.

The door kicks open and framed against a pale light is Shawn. "What'cha, Tobias," he hisses, pronouncing the last syllable of my name as arse. "Don't you have school tomorrow?" There's another loud clunk, which is followed by a rustling sound.

I push myself up onto my elbows to see better. He has a large object under his arm. "What you got there?"

Shawn puffs out his cheeks, and backs into my room. Whatever it is he's holding, it's too wide to go through the door. "Flick your light on," he says in a half-whisper, "and I'll permit you to have a gander."

I reach over to my bedside table, feel for the switch, and flood the room with light. I shield my eyes, but I can still see that he is carrying a long object wrapped in two or more black bin liners.

"Shift your plates of meat," says Shawn. I pull my feet up under the covers to make space and he plants himself at the foot of my bed with the object across his knees. "You are not going to believe what I've got." He gives off a low growl that turns into a deep rollicking laugh. *Wooar-haw-haw-haw!*

I push myself up into a full sitting position. "You going to show me or just leave me to guess?"

Shawn tilts his head toward me. "Sometimes, Tobias, talking to you is like talking to Mom." He burps, then sways for a moment. "Get a load of this." He draws off the first bag, revealing the neck of an electric bass.

My pulse quickens so fast I'm almost knocked over by the G-force. "Bloody hell, Shawn! That's a Fender."

He pauses with the second bag half off. "Yeah. I know what it is."

"It's just about the best electric bass that money can buy," I say. Even though I don't want to, I lean forward and reach out to touch it. The yellow-colored wood of the headstock is as smooth as a kitten's stomach. "These are worth a fortune."

"Keep your hair on," says Shawn. "It's old, for starters, plus the electrics need a bit of attention." He finally peels off the second bag, exposing the whole instrument.

I can't contain a gasp.

"It is a bit like seeing a bird in her birthday suit, innit?" Shawn leers at me.

"I don't know if I'd go that far," I say, although the instrument really is sexy, for want of a better word. The deep oranges and reds glint, and the yellowing chrome reflects shafts like laser beams across the ceiling.

"Not that you would know, of course." He reaches over and squeezes my knee. "Not yet, of course." He does his growling laugh again, *Wooar-haw-haw-haw!* "Depends on the bird in question, I suppose."

"I've seen a few," I say.

"I meant a real one," he says. "Not a photo." He tilts the bass into a playing position across his knees and plucks a note, although it's more of a flat clunk than a note. "Or am I mis-underestimating you?"

I fold my forearms across my knees as if the question is beneath me.

"Here. Have a listen." Shawn plays. What follows is

not so much a stream of booming bass notes, but more of a series of clacks and squeaks. "Recognize it?"

I have to be diplomatic here. "The Stones, right?" I tilt my head as if I'm concentrating. "I think it's one I don't know."

"Close," he says. "Beatles."

"Oh. Right," I say. "Umm..."

"'Nowhere Man,'" says Shawn.

"I was just about to say that."

"Here," he says. "Show us how it's done." He balances it across his palms and places it in my lap.

"What do you want me to play?" I say.

Shawn pushes his hands together into a prayer position. "Play something you learned in your guitar lessons."

"I'm working on a Bach piece. He didn't write a lot of material for electric bass."

I could explain to him that this instrument is not really a guitar, but Shawn would just view this as a feeble excuse. I shift the bass. It's a lot heavier than I expected, about as heavy as a three-and-a-half-foot-long piece of lumber. I lay my fingers on the strings and push down. The fat strings are much harder to push down than the strings on my classical guitar. I play a scale, and then go into a movement from Bach's Canticle in E minor. It actually sounds pretty good on the bass.

"There you go," says Shawn. "'Nowhere Man.' Sounds like you've been playing it for years."

"'Nowhere Man'?" I say. "It's Bach."

"Hah," says Shawn. "Sounds exactly like Paul McCartney's bass line to me. That Bach bloke ought to sue him."

"Well…" I go back to the start and play the figure again. "He's been pushing up the daisies for about four hundred years." Not only am I getting used to the thick strings, I'm actually beginning to like this instrument.

"You know, if I was going to give up playing classical and make the switch to pop music," I say, "which I'm not," I slide my fingers up the neck, which makes a sort of whooping sound, "this is what I'd play."

Shawn is still bobbing his head to the rhythm of the tune I stopped playing a couple of minutes ago. "You're a natural."

I noodle some random notes. "So where did you get it?"

Shawn lets out a long sigh. "I paid for it, if that's what your asking," he says. "It's mine."

He nods as if I've said something to cast doubt, which I haven't.

"Did you buy it from a shop?" I say.

Shawn does his rollicking laugh, *Wooar-haw-haw-haw!* and shakes his head. "I bought it off some plonker in Brunswick." He reaches over and retrieves the bass.

I don't really want to give it back, but then, as he says, it is his.

"I've got to tell you," he says. He starts noodling random notes up and down the strings. "The moment I handed over the cash I had second thoughts." Noodle, noodle. "But the bloke I bought it off? He was a scary-looking bastard. Not a big bloke. But still scary, if you know what I mean. Once I'd given him the money, that was it. A done deal. No going back."

I nod as if I know exactly what he means, but I don't really. Shawn is big and handy. It's the first time I've ever heard him say he was scared of someone. "How much did you pay for it?" I say.

Shawn stops playing and props the bass on the floor. "Five hundred," he says.

"Five hundred pounds?" I say.

"No, five hundred Tiddly Winks," he says. "Keep your voice down. I don't want to wake Mom."

"Where did you get five hundred pounds?" I whisper.

"I've been doing a lot of overtime at the chip shop," he says.

"That's a heck of a lot of overtime," I say. "I thought you only got ten pounds an hour."

"You get double after six," he says. "Triple after ten." He nods. "It adds up fast."

"Can I work there?" I say. "I wouldn't mind making thirty quid an hour."

Shawn squeezes my knee again. "I'll ask," he says. "I'll put a word in for you." He gathers up the bags and wraps them around the bass.

"Can I borrow it?" I say.

Shawn does his laugh. "Use it all you want," he says. "But I have one stipulation."

"I'll take really good care of it," I say.

"I'm not worried about that," he says. "My stipulation is that you don't take it to school, and you don't brag about it."

"Is that all?" I say.

"I'm serious, Toby," he says. He only calls me Toby when he's serious. "I don't really want you shooting your mouth off about it."

"Why?" I say.

Shawn looks down at the floor. "It's valuable. I don't want to risk someone coming in and stealing it."

"We can insure it, right?" I say.

Shawn looks over at the door. "I have to find out," he says. "I think there might be a problem with the serial number."

With that he rolls back up to his feet and moves toward the door. "Hit the light," he says. "Go to sleep. You can play with it in the morning."

18
SATURDAY

"Toby! My man!"

I open my eyes to find Zack standing over me with his wet hair plastered to his head. He's in the middle of unbuttoning his blue denim jacket, which is so wet that it's almost black. He slides it off, holds it up for a second as if he's looking for a hanger, then lets it thump to the floor.

"Hey," I say. "My man." I try to sit up, but I can't. Then I realize I have the bass on my chest. For a second I'm happy, thinking Shawn is still here, then the memory of the last hour trickles back into my head.

"Come on. Time is money. Last rehearsal." Zack steps

across to the bed and lifts the bass off my chest. He spins it around and strums it as if it's a guitar, which sounds awful, and about as sad as I feel. He slides his fingers right up the fretboard, then strums it as if it's a banjo. He croons his version of the old Rod Stewart song. "Wake up, Toby, I really should be getting back to school..."

I groan.

"What's up with you then?" Zack props the bass up in the corner. "You're looking more-than-usually bummed out."

I think about everything I want to tell him. This isn't going to be easy. Maybe it's best to leave it for now.

"Come on, let's play." I push myself off the bed and fetch the bass from the corner. "Let's run through the set."

What follows is the usual setting-up routine, and a minute later we're standing there with our guitars. Zack counts us in, but before I even play the first note of "Ticket to Ride" I flop back down onto the bed.

"Listen, mate." I pluck a string then slide my finger down the fret board, making a sinking sound. "I can't do this."

"Can't do what?" Zack strums a soft E minor chord. "Can't do the gig? Can't rehearse?"

"There's some shit I have to tell you." I lay the bass flat on my knees and rest my elbows on the body. "I can't avoid telling you."

"Okay. What's eating you, mate?" Zack puts the guitar back in its case, stumbles over to the bed, then flops back against the wall next to me. "Something happened, right? Wait. You didn't do anything stupid like phone that dingbat in Brunswick again?"

"He rang back, actually, but I'd ring my dad before I ring him again." There's no way to lead into this so I just come right out with it. "It's not about the bloke in Brunswick, it's about Shawn. He's in the Glasshouse," I say.

"Bloody hell. The Glasshouse!" Zack leaps away from the wall, then freezes. "Wait a minute. What's the Glasshouse?"

"It's the Navy prison." I twiddle the controls on the bass. "It's in Colchester, just outside London."

"Bloody heck!" Zack sweeps his hair behind his ears. "How long is he in for?" He leans sideways on the wall, then turns and leans flat again. "I mean, what did he do?"

"I don't know what he did." I stand up and prop the bass against the amp. "Well, actually, he stole something, but I don't know what it was." I flop back on the bed. "He has to have a court-martial, but that's not the most important point." I lean back against the wall and pull my knees into my chest. "The important thing is that Mom wants to go back to London now."

"Holy crap." Zack jumps off the bed and walks around the room with his hands in his pockets. "Oh, Toby. Man. That's absolute pants," he says. "Why?"

I take a long breath. "Shawn's going to have the court-martial there," I say. "They tend to give long sentences. It might be our last chance to see him for a while."

Zack pulls his John Lennon glasses out of his pocket and puts them on. "I thought you couldn't afford to go back."

"We can't," I say. "We'll have to go into debt, but hopefully Mom will make some money fairly quickly when we get there so we can pay it off."

"So, you're not coming back here again?" he says.

I shake my head.

"When are you going?" Zack folds his arms and rocks back and forth.

"Next Wednesday," I say.

"Bloody nora," says Zack. "But wait." He takes the guitar out of its case, props it upright on the floor, and leans on it. "It's not the end of the world. We could still keep the band going. London's not that far."

"It's a nice idea," I say. "I did actually think about it, but how would we make it work? We don't have cars, and we can't afford the train."

"It's not long till you can get your license." Zack puts the guitar strap over his shoulder, and takes the pick out from between the strings. "You could borrow your mum's Toyota."

"It's still a while till I can drive," I say.

Zack snaps his fingers. "Bicycles," he says. "You ride north. I ride south. We meet in the middle."

"We could practice over the phone," I say. "Just put the receiver on a table and play into it."

"Brilliant." Zack softly strums the descending chords

sequence to "Michelle," of all songs. "We could play after six o'clock when the rates go down."

"It's barely going to be a problem at all," I say. "We could even do gigs by phone."

"Yeah. Pipe dreams." Zack puts his foot up on the bed and strums "Yesterday." "We'll do this one gig. Maybe we can get another one the next day and make it two gigs before we break up."

"Please." I point to Zack's strumming fingers. "Would you mind not playing that one. It's just too depressing right now."

"Sorry. I know. It's depressing at almost any time." Zack switches and plinks out the melody to "Penny Lane." "Maybe we could practice once a month or something."

"Unfortunately I'm not going to have this anymore." I slap the body of the bass like it's a bongo drum in time to what Zack's playing.

"Wait." Zack stops playing in the middle of a bar. "I thought we went through all that and you were going to keep it."

"Yeah. I know." I flip the bass into playing position and absent-mindedly noodle some scales. "But I had a change of heart."

"What brought that on?" says Zack.

"Well, there's this girl," I say.

"Blimey O'Reilly." Zack cranks out a spooky power chord. "How many wars have started with the phrase, *There's this girl?*" he says. "When did this happen?"

"Her name's Michelle," I say. "I met her at the Aquarium."

"Michelle? Bloody heck," says Zack. "I always knew you were a dark horse, but I didn't realize you were that dark." He goes back to strumming "Michelle." "So what happened? You going to run off to London with her?" He switches to "The Long and Winding Road." "Is all this stuff about Shawn just a cock-and-bull story?"

"I wish," I say. "I mean I wish it wasn't true that Shawn was in the slammer." I play the bass along with what Zack's playing. "I don't really want to run off to London with this girl. I mean she's nice and all. Actually, I don't even know that she is nice, really. She's alright I suppose. She just has a bit of attitude."

"Wait a minute." Zack stops playing. "This is bringing on a touch of the old déjà vu. She's not the vertically challenged one from Portland Road, is she?"

"I suppose you could say that." I play the verse to "Blackbird."

"So she was the one who tracked you down, then." Zack joins in quietly with the chords. "Bloody nora. Did she just breathe down the front of your shirt and say, 'Oh, Toby, if you give back the bass I will make you a very happy young man'?"

"Not in so many words," I say. "No."

"Did she change your mind with her mind-numbing power of rhetoric?" he says. "Or did she pour you a drink and slip into something more comfortable?"

"Um…" I say. "It was closer to the first thing you said."

"The rhetoric?" says Zack.

"Yeah," I say. "It was mostly rhetoric."

"She didn't promise you a little tussle under the jelly-fish tank?" says Zack.

"We didn't even look at the jellyfish." I play the chorus of "Blackbird." "Actually she was up here, sitting more or less exactly where your foot is right now."

"Whoa!" Zack leaps away from the bed, then turns around and examines the spot in question. "I thought I noticed an unfamiliar bum imprint."

"Look," I say. "The phone number was useless, so I'm going to take the bus to Brunswick tomorrow. See if I can find Julie McGuire that way. If she deserves to get the bass back, then I'll keep it to play the gig on Monday, and I'll take it back on Tuesday."

"I didn't mean to be a wet rag," says Zack. "Seriously, if you want my help, then let me know. I'll go to Brunswick with you. We can track this Julie down together."

"I appreciate it," I say, "but I think Michelle's going to go with me. She lives in Brunswick."

"Woo-hoo," says Zack. "Fancy that. Port Jackson girls aren't good enough for you anymore?"

"No. It's just that they're all lusting after you, mate," I say.

"They just have sophisticated taste," says Zack.

"Yeah," I say. "That's what makes it so puzzling."

"Are you going to play that thing?" Zack prods the

bass with his toe. "Because if you're not, then we might as well take it back right now."

"I need to ask you one huge favor," I say.

"How could I deny you anything?" Zack adjusts the strap on his shoulder, and plugs the lead into the amp. "Wait. Don't tell me. We have to play 'Michelle' now."

"Not quite," I say. "'Blackbird.'"

"'Blackbird'?" Zack swivels his mouth around as if he's trying to get something out from between his teeth. "Pick an easy one, why don't you."

"I just worked out the bass line," I say. "It's pretty easy."

"Yeah. The bass line is easy," says Zack. "My part is another story. The guitar chords from hell. What does it start with? G diminished minor suspended off Tower Bridge?"

19
SATURDAY

After we work out "Blackbird," we just plow straight through the rest of the set: "Ticket to Ride," "Can't Buy Me Love," "Tell Me Why," "Get Back," "I Should Have Known Better," "Revolution," "Eight Days a Week," "Lady Madonna," and "Day Tripper."

One song just leads straight into the other.

The set sounds great as it is, but after a little discussion we decide to put "Blackbird" in third, instead of "Tell Me Why."

Working any more on the songs is pointless. We don't

need any more rehearsal and call it a day, even though it's earlier than usual.

Zack offers to stay, but I'd rather be left alone, and I know he really wants to go. Probably off to write some steamy letter to Bethany, and then wax down his surfboard. As soon as I hear the downstairs door bang shut, I put the bass away, crash back on Shawn's bed, and try to hang on to the upbeat feeling I got from playing through the set.

I do this by trying to imagine what it's going to be like when we play at Jubilee. It doesn't really work though, and after a couple of minutes I roll off the bed and start fiddling around with the bass again.

"Blackbird" sounds fine, but I could use a little more practice, so I pull out the Fake Book, and flip through the pages until I come to it. I hum through the melody, and then work my way through the chord progression. It should make me think about Michelle, but it doesn't. Instead it makes me think about Shawn.

He's in prison, and I don't feel anything. Does that make me a bad person?

Shawn was definitely no Robin Hood. Sure, he never took any tangible things from me. Not only that, he gave me things like the bass. But he stole something far more important.

When he did whatever it was he did, he robbed me of my last two months in Port Jackson.

Being robbed of time in Port Jackson might not normally seem like a bad thing, but he's taken a couple of months with the band, just as we've started playing in public. Who knows where that would have led?

Worse than that, he's robbed me of time with Michelle. Could that relationship survive me moving to London? Not a five-day relationship. Definitely not, but maybe a two-month one could survive as one of those long-distance things.

Nice work, Shawn. Good one. Three years I've been here, most of the time as a total hermit, and then the minute I get a life, you take it away from me.

Now I have to deal with the fallout.

I've told Zack we're leaving, and that was hard enough. Now I have to tell Michelle.

I play out the scene in my head. She'll come to Brunswick with me. She'll be all happy to see me; she'll probably give me a big kiss, and then I'll have to tell her.

I wish I could tell her right now and get it over with. I don't really want to wait till tomorrow to tell her what's happened, and the more I think about it, the more I realize that I don't actually have to. There's no reason why I couldn't go and see her, but if I'm going to go over there, I have to go right now.

I scoot down the stairs three at a time. According to the clock above the kitchen door, it's 7:57. Mom will be home in three minutes. I have to leave before she comes in. If I wait till after she gets home then I'll have to provide a long explanation of why and where I'm going. Even on a normal day she doesn't really like me going out after it gets dark. By the time I'm through with the explanation and the negotiations, it really will be too late to go out. I'll have to tell Mom where I've been when I get back, but by then I will have done what I need to do.

For the first time since I heard the news about Shawn, I actually feel a little better. I waste one valuable minute checking myself out in the bathroom mirror. There's nothing that plastic surgery can't fix, but now I only have two minutes left to get out of the house.

I grab my jacket, swing through the front door, and leap down all three steps of the stoop in one go.

I could either go north along Gray Street or south along Brackett Street. I spy a tall woman carrying a purple umbrella walking up Winter Street. My mother.

Then it hits me. The umbrella. Michelle's umbrella. It's the perfect excuse to go over and make a spur-of-the-moment visit. But now it's too late. Mom is fifty yards from the end of the driveway. I take a step toward Michelle's house, then a step home, and I think I might even scream aloud in frustration. Arrrggh! I hurtle back up the driveway, fishing the keys out of my pocket as I run. I shoot through the door, grab the umbrella, and bound back down the driveway to Winter Street. I know I'm too late. I've blown it. I know I will run straight into Mom on the driveway, but I get all the way to the pavement without seeing her. I glance in the direction I last saw her.

A van is pulling out of another driveway fifty yards down. Mom is nowhere to be seen. She must be on the other side of the van. Without a second thought I pound up Winter Street as I fast as I can, and I don't rest until I'm halfway to Spring Street. I slow down to catch my breath next to the big chestnut tree at the corner of Gray and Spring Streets. Not so much of a rush now that I'm actually out of the house.

As I pass the chestnut tree I'm stopped in my tracks by a long, wailing hoot. It's somewhere between the sound of train whistle and the sound it makes when you blow across the top of an empty bottle. It's the loneliest sound I've ever heard, and it's also a familiar sound.

At least it's a sound I've heard hundreds of times before, and never thought twice about, but this evening is different. Naturally, there are no trains in the higher branches of the chestnut tree and by a quick process of elimination I figure out that it's an owl.

I suppose that for an expert it would be more than just an owl. It would be a greater, spotted, or crested owl, but now I have yet another excuse to call on Michelle. I can tell her about the owl.

Now I've recovered from my running escape from Winter Street, I try to predict how it's going to go.

I'll ring the bell.

Her dad will answer.

I will explain about the owl.

He will be very interested and impressed that I spotted an owl. He will call Michelle. She'll be a little surprised, and a little shocked.

I'm going to have to tell her my news that I'm leaving the moment she comes to the door. If I delay it even for a moment she's going to be all smiling, and happy, and pleased to see me, and then I won't be able to tell her.

My walk slows down to an amble, and from an amble, to a shuffle. Maybe I shouldn't do this now. But I'm here. I'm at the corner of Spring Street. By now, Michelle might have seen me from a window if she just happened to be looking out. She's going to be really confused if I'm wandering around outside. She'll think I'm a stalker, whereas in reality I'm really the exact opposite.

I check the address on the umbrella tag, and make my way up the garden path. I pause for one moment to run my fingers through my hair, then I jog up the three steps to the front door. A light spills through a diamond-shaped window in the door.

Good, they're home.

Below the window is a brass knocker.

I'm just about to use the knocker when I notice that there's a bell on the doorpost. I get the urge to push the button and hold it for a while, but I just do a quick buzz. I don't want to sound aggressive like my dad. I don't want to be right in the face of whoever is going to come to the door, so I step back down to the pathway.

I've rolled the umbrella badly, so I unfurl it and roll it up again. I double-check the zipper on my trousers and force it right up to my belt. But nobody comes. Now I have the longing to ring the bell again. To fight the temptation, I wander back down to the pavement. This also gives me the chance to take in the whole front of the house. The only light is the one in the hall. Don't they say that leaving the hall light on is a sure signal to burglars that there's nobody home?

Rats! They've gone out. I've spent all this effort building myself up for this, and now I'm going to have to tell her tomorrow anyway. I suppose if they're out then there's no harm in ringing the bell a second time. I make my way back up to the door and up the steps. Just as I'm about to press the bell, a voice behind me says, "Can I help you?" in a tone that sounds somewhat unhelpful.

20
SATURDAY

I spin around and come face-to-face with a tall, heavyset man. He's about three or four paces behind me, lurking in the shadows of the front garden. I have no idea how long he's been standing there. He must have come around from the back of the house in complete silence, because I heard nothing.

This must be a trick he learned from defending himself against charging bulls.

He must have also been doing some late gardening, because clutched in one hand is a large fork.

Or perhaps he's about to use the fork on me.

Maybe he thinks I'm a burglar.

"Is Michelle home?" I say. I'm actually impressed by how steady my voice is.

I'm not sure that speaking to him helps, because he shifts the fork into his opposite hand, and now the prongs are pointed directly at my throat.

"I'm Toby," I say in my most un-burglarish voice.

He gives a short laugh, says, "I know perfectly well who you are," and steps forward into the yellowish glow of the street lamp.

I'm so shocked I actually have the urge to scream. Luckily, my throat goes so dry that the scream comes out as a kind of choke.

I have to reach back and steady myself against the front door.

Michelle Frost! Of course. How daft could I be.

I've often been accused of being slow on the uptake, but I don't think I've ever been this slow before.

That's why she was at the Aquarium.

That's why she was at the rugby game.

She wasn't there to see Jasper Hamilton-Sinclair.

She was there to see her dad: Frosty.

The same Frosty who is now looking at me as if I've come here with the sole purpose of stealing everything in his house.

"Good evening, Mr. Frost, sir," I say in a voice that gets less steady with each word. "I'm actually friends with Michelle. Is she home?"

At the mention of Michelle's name his expression transforms completely. He goes from looking at me like I'm a burglar to looking at me like I'm a rapist.

"What is it you want?" he bellows, as if I'm a quarter of a mile away from him, instead of a couple of feet. "Holland!"

This is probably the same tone that he uses to scare off charging bulls.

"I'm sorry to bother you, sir," I say, not quite as confidently as I would like. "She lent me this." I hold up the umbrella. He keeps his eyes fixed on me, and doesn't look at what's in my hand. Maybe he doesn't realize I'm talking about the umbrella.

"It was raining this afternoon," I say by way of further explanation—although, off the top of my head, I can't think of any other reason why someone would lend out an umbrella.

I glance from his face to the umbrella, then back to his face.

My fear level begins to escalate. Maybe he's not slow on the uptake. Maybe there's some other reason why he's not responding. Maybe he's considering different methods of slaughtering me.

The umbrella's getting heavy in my hand. Just as I lower my arm, he reaches out and grabs it from me. I'm not quite sure how this happens, as I don't remember moving, but the next thing I know, he's standing between me and the door, clutching both the fork and the umbrella in the same large fist.

"Thank you," he says, in the same tone that he might have said "if I see you here again I will kill you."

Now I have the urge to say goodbye, turn, and run back down the path to Gray Street, but I stand my ground. I take a deep breath. "Is she home?" I say.

His expression shifts slightly. "No," he says. "She's gone out."

I'm about to tell him it's been a pleasure and leave when I actually begin to feel a little angry. Even though I'm terrified of this person, I actually take a step toward him. "Will she be back soon?" I say.

"She will not," he says. "Holland."

"Oh. Okay," I say. "Maybe I'll come back tomorrow."

"She won't be here tomorrow," he says. "Holland."

I'm just about to suggest next week, when he says, "I hate to be the one to break the news, Holland." He shakes his head. "She doesn't want to see you again."

I say, "But I was just with her a couple of hours ago—"

"Holland," he says.

I look up at his face, and all of the hostility has gone. His eyes are crinkled into a smile, but it's not a friendly smile. More of a triumphant smirk.

"Good evening, Holland," he says. "I will see you tomorrow at school."

What would Shawn do? Shawn would let out a big laugh, slap Mister Frost on the back, and within a minute the two of them would be best buddies. Frosty would say where Michelle had gone. If it was Shawn, Frosty would probably even give Shawn a ride to meet her.

No. Who am I kidding? Shawn would put one hand around Frosty's shoulder and lift his wallet with the other.

What do I do? I say ,"Yes, sir," and let out a long, ragged breath and head back down the path to Gray Street.

21
SUNDAY

Horoscope: April 18, Aquarius:
Act on the spur of the moment to create
new pizzazz in your life. Why not try a new
hairstyle? Throw caution to the wind and
do the unexpected.

"I suppose I could live with being called the Sand Tigers for one gig," says Zack, as we climb off the bus.

"I know it's not the perfect name." This is so strange to me that all I can do is stand on the asphalt and stare. There's about a thousand people milling around. "It's just better than all of the other names we've come up with." It feels like there are more people in the Brunswick bus station than in all of Port Jackson. "I wish Michelle was here," I say. "If she was it would be a breeze."

A group of Hare Krishnas make their way along the

pavement a few yards away from us, chanting and playing drums as they go.

"Hah. Michelle Frost," says Zack. "Who would have thought that Frosty would have such a pretty daughter? Come to think of it, who would have thought he would have kids at all? Can you imagine having him as a dad?"

I squeeze my eyes shut.

"What are you doing?" says Zack.

"I'm imagining having Frosty as a dad," I say. "It's actually not as bad as you might think."

"Is there some level at which you can take this business seriously," says Zack. "I'm here because of you. Given the choice I'd rather be at home in bed. If it was my bass, I'd keep it."

"It's Sunday morning," I say, opening my eyes. "If you were a half-decent human being you'd be in church." Over Zack's shoulder I see a girl with long, dark hair, looking at the bus timetables. "Look. Over there!" I point at the girl.

"It's my humanity that keeps me away from church." Zack twists around to look in the direction I'm pointing. "If I suddenly showed up, the pew people would get confused and think it was Christmas. You know, midnight mass being the only time I ever set foot in a church." He glances back at me. "What am I looking at?"

"It's Michelle." I keep my eyes on her. "I know it's a weird coincidence, but it's her. I'm sure of it."

Zack looks back and shakes his head. "Not unless she's aged twenty-five years. She looks about forty." He punches me on the shoulder. "I still don't understand why you couldn't persuade Frosty to give you Michelle's address in Brunswick."

"He was about to shove a garden fork up my arse," I say. "It kind of slipped my mind to ask him."

The girl turns to face us, revealing the thin and lined face of a woman.

"I see what you mean," I say.

"So, do you actually have some kind of a plan?" says Zack.

The Hare Krishnas move away, and as they do they reveal another dark-haired female. Her hair is swinging side to side as she approaches.

I know she's not Michelle, but I can't stop staring at her until I'm absolutely certain.

"I mean, how are we going to find Julie McGuire?" says Zack. "Toby?" He leans sideways, placing himself between me and the girl. He turns to look, then he turns back to me. "Toby," he says again.

"It's okay," I say. "I know it's not her."

"Please stop," says Zack. "She's not here. Anyway," he continues, "a plan? You're taking us on a trip to nowhere. I realize that we're called the Nowhere Men, but it's just a name. We don't always have to be going nowhere."

"I thought we'd decided on the Sand Tigers as a name." I point to the wall where I'd just seen the person who wasn't Michelle. "There's a map. Let's find where Mariner Street is, then we'll be somewhere."

"The Sand Tigers is okay," says Zack, as we make our way through the crowd toward the map. "But if we call ourselves the Nowhere Men, then people will know we do Beatles stuff."

"I'm not saying I don't like the Nowhere Men." I immediately find the bus station on the map. There's a spot right in the middle of the map that's worn away from a thousand people prodding it and going *We're here,* so I prod the map, and say, "We're here." Then I turn to Zack. "Why did you say you liked the Sand Tigers when we were on the bus if you didn't like it?"

"I didn't say I liked it." Zack runs his finger along the map from the worn-out spot. "Look. St. James Street, Eastern Road, Norfolk Square, Mariner Street. Looks pretty easy." He turns to me. "I said I thought I could live with it for one gig."

Both of us make it across the six lanes of St. James Street, and we turn left. Eastern Road is lined with shops that are either out of business or just about to go out of business.

An empty glass bottle is propped on the curb right next to a garbage can. "Anyway," I say as I reach down and put the bottle in the garbage. "Why are things different now? What's changed in—I don't know—four minutes?"

"You're quite forceful," says Shawn. "I don't think you realize it."

"So, you mean you didn't really like the name," I say, as we turn in to Norfolk Square and begin walking around it in a clockwise direction. A wiry-looking woman passes us. She has dyed orange hair and a cigarette dangling from her thin lips.

I can't help staring at her for a moment.

"She's not Michelle," says Zack.

I shake my head. I can't think of a better response.

The shops on Norfolk Square look pretty dingy, but we must be moving toward a better neighborhood because at least some of the shops are still in business.

"I'm not saying I don't like the Nowhere Men," I say.

"I'm not saying I'm completely averse to the Sand Tigers," says Zack.

"So which is it going to be?" I say. "A compromise? The Sand Men? The Nowhere Tigers?"

Finally we reach Mariner Street. I've already had one culture shock this morning traveling from the sleepy seaside town of Port Jackson to the metropolis of Brunswick. It's almost as big a shock to turn off Norfolk Square onto a side street. There couldn't be more of a contrast between the shabby and derelict Norfolk Square and the big, fancy houses of Mariner Street. I would guess that the people who live here don't do their shopping on Norfolk Square.

The only thing the two streets have in common is that they're both deserted.

"Do you know how many people live in Brunswick?" says Zack. "Almost half a million. Have you got that?"

"Look, we're on the right side." I point to the numbers on the houses. "There's two, and there's four. We're on the right track." The houses aren't a lot bigger than our house on Winter Street, except that each one has a big front and backyard. All of the houses look recently painted, but the big difference is in the cars. Winter Street is lined with battered and dented wrecks. The cars parked on Mariner Street are all shiny Mercedeses and BMWs.

"Okay." Zack turns to me. "If we make any progress on finding this Julie person, then I will let you choose the name."

"Deal," I say. "If Julie McGuire lives here," I point at the cars, "do you think she's too rich to even care about the bass?"

"The chances are that Julie McGuire is no longer Julie McGuire," says Zack. "The note might have been written years ago, so now she's probably got herself married and she's Julie something else. Julie is a pretty common name. How many Julies do you think live in Brunswick? Hundreds, probably."

We reach number forty, and I can't help slowing down as I realize the seriousness of what I'm about to do. For the second time in less than twenty-four hours, I'm about to ring the doorbell and not know what to expect. The last time wasn't exactly a runaway success.

"There you go," says Zack. "48."

We come to a stop outside a house with a front garden so perfect it probably gets manicured with nail scissors.

"Doesn't look too much like the abode of an aging bass player," I say.

"That's just what I'm trying to tell you," says Zack.

"Julie McGuire is no longer Julie McGuire. New name. Totally different life. Anyway, we need 48B."

The next house is number fifty. We walk back past forty-eight, and the next house in that direction is forty-six. We walk back to forty-eight.

"Maybe 48B is behind 48," says Zack. "You know sometimes people build a house in their back garden."

"We can't just walk into 48's garden," I say.

"I'll do it," says Zack. "There's nobody about to see me."

Just as Zack stops speaking a door slams across the street. A few moments later a heavyset bloke emerges from a driveway about ten houses down, and crosses to our side. A tiny Pekingese kind of dog is running along beside him on the end of a leash.

"Let this bloke go past," I say. As he gets closer I can see that he's just a very big kid, not much older than us.

"Typical," says Zack. "As soon as you don't want anyone around, then someone appears."

"Wait," I say. "Why don't we just ask him?"

The bloke stops about four houses down while his dog does its dog thing, but as soon as the dog is finished they do an about turn and head away from us.

"Come on," I say to Zack. "It's our best chance." I stumble into a jog. Zack falls in behind, and then passes me. As we get closer, something begins to feel a little familiar about this kid with the dog. The kid crosses the street and is just about to go back into his driveway when Zack sprints ahead.

"Hang on a second," I say to him.

But Zack doesn't hear me. He runs right up to the kid, who's a good head taller than Zack. "Excuse me," he says.

The kid turns, and I choke.

"Goodness me," says the kid, looking from Zack to me and then back again. "It's the two bra straps from Port Jackson."

"Hi Jasper," I say.

"You're calling us bra straps?" Zack points to the dog. "That's not exactly a Rottweiler you've got there, is it?"

Please stop, I mutter under my breath. This is not the best way to approach Jasper Hamilton-Sinclair.

22
SUNDAY

"Jasper, old pal." I say this in my most diplomatic voice, while his pooch lunges and snarls at me. "Can you tell us where forty-eight B is?"

Jasper blows out a raspberry. "What on earth are you doing here?" He reels in his dog like he's reeling in a prize haddock. "Aside from which, what do you want to know for?"

"Listen." Zack bends down and holds out his fingers for the dog to sniff, but it just growls and snaps at him. "We're trying to do something good and decent, and we're just asking for your help."

"If you don't want to help," I move out of the dog's range as it circles around Jasper, making exasperated grunts, "then we can go somewhere else," I say.

"But if that is the case," says Zack, "we won't be able to offer you any guarantees that news about the manly kind of dog you keep as a pet won't spread around the school."

"She's not my dog," says Jasper. "She's my mum's."

"We understand that," says Zack, "but not everyone else is going to see the subtleties of the situation."

The pooch squats down and does its thing again, then kicks backward with its little legs.

"Look. Why don't you come in?" Jasper walks backward toward the house he originally came out of. "My dad will be back from the station soon and I'm supposed to set the table for lunch."

"In?" says Zack. "You mean to your house?"

"Yes. I live in a house," says Jasper. "This isn't Port Jackson. We stopped living in caves a couple of years ago."

"Very witty," says Zack.

We follow Jasper across his trim lawn and in through the front door, where we're surrounded by the smell of roast beef.

I can't help feeling a little hungry. "I think Zack's upset," I say to Jasper. I lower my voice. "He really does live in a cave."

"Sorry," says Jasper in a fake whisper as he unhooks the dog from its lead. "I won't mention it again."

"Are you talking about me?" says Zack as he closes the

door behind us. "It's ironic, isn't it? You're the Neanderthal," he says to Jasper, "and I'm the one who lives in a cave."

"Do you want my help or not?" says Jasper.

"Yeah. Sorry," I say to him as he guides us through to the kitchen. I start to sketch out the details, leaving out as much as I can. "There's this bass."

"We found it," says Zack.

"It seems like it was probably stolen," I say. "It had a note inside saying it belonged to a Julie McGuire at 48B Mariner Street."

"Which is right opposite you," says Zack.

"Or should be," I say, "but isn't, and we want to give it back."

Jasper doesn't seem to react to what I've told him. Instead he puts on oven gloves, squats down, and checks on whatever is cooking. The smell of roast meat is barely endurable.

"So," he says. "Julie McGuire at 48B." He pulls out a drawer next to the sink, and gathers up a handful of knives and forks. "Interesting." He hands me the bundle of eating tools. "Could you take those through to the dining room?" He indicates an archway next to the fridge.

"Um. Sure," I say.

He opens a cupboard and pulls out a pile of plates and hands them to Zack.

"Gee, thanks," says Zack.

Jasper gathers up some glasses and then we go into a long room with tall windows, in the middle of which is a dark wooden table. Jasper goes ahead of us and drops three place mats in front of three chairs at one end of the table, then puts the glasses in front of them.

"I hope you're making us do this because you have some information," says Zack, holding the plates in front of his chest.

Jasper points to Zack and then to the mats. "You can put one of those on each of these." He slides rolled-up napkins next to them. "I actually think I might know the very person you're talking about."

"So where's 48B?" I say.

"Just put the knives and forks next to the plates, Toby," says Jasper. "48 used to have a flat on the top floor."

I place a knife and a fork next to the plate at the head of the table.

"No, you nincompoop." Jasper grabs the silverware out of my hand. "Knife on the right, fork on the left."

"Sorry," I say.

"What I can't say for certain," Jasper places three more mats, this time down the centre of the table, "is that it was called 48B."

"Is there another Mariner Street in Brunswick?" I say.

"There are dozens of them, Toby," says Jasper. "Makes it easy for the post office." He takes a salt and pepper from a side table under a painting of someone dressed up as an admiral. "Let's assume that the house across the street is the one in the note." He makes a gap in between two of the mats to make room for the salt and pepper.

"So does Julie McGuire still live there?" says Zack. "Is it that simple?"

Jasper shakes his head. "At one point there was a girl living there." He moves around the table, switching the knives and forks from left to right. "I suppose you'd call her a woman really, but she was very pretty. I never knew what her name was, but what makes me think it might be her is that she played the guitar."

"But did she play the bass?" I say.

Jasper pulls out the chair at the head of table. "You can sit down for a moment if you like."

Both Zack and I pull out chairs and sit.

"There was this one summer," says Jasper, picking up the knife and fork in front of him. "I don't know if you noticed it, but forty-eight has a balcony." He holds the knife and fork like drumsticks, and begins tapping out a four-four beat on the place mat. "She used to sit out there and play. I used to see her every evening on the way home from school." He does a drumroll with the knife and fork then goes back to the four-four. "I was just a kid. I didn't know the difference between an electric guitar and an electric bass. But. Yeah. Could easily have been a bass." He does a final roll, then pings the knife on the glass.

"That was nice," I say, pointing to the knife and fork.

Jasper looks puzzled for a second then looks down at the knife and fork. "Oh. Thanks," he says. He places the utensils back next to the mat. "I've got to tell you one thing. She was a lot older than me."

"It has to be her," says Zack. "How much older was she?"

"I used to have wet dreams about her," says Jasper, adjusting the knife and fork so they line up perfectly.

"This is much more information than we were expecting," says Zack.

Jasper glares at him with one eyebrow raised. "I used to have to walk past my mother's bedroom every morning to go to the bathroom." He folds his arms. "I had to keep my hands folded in front of my crotch."

I squeeze my eyes shut in an attempt to stop any unwanted images drifting into my mind. "Jasper," I say, "do you know where she might have gone when she moved?"

He shakes his head. "It was awful," he says with a long sigh. "I spent every day at school trying to pluck up the courage to speak to her, and then one day I actually did it." He looks from me to Zack. "It was crazy. She must have been twenty years older than me. But I was in love." He folds his arms and looks down at his feet again. "I snuck out of the house while my parents were watching the news. I wanted to run, but I walked calmly over there and rang the doorbell." He puts his head in hands and goes quiet for a moment.

"I remember standing there," he says, "straightening my clothes and brushing my hair with my fingers. Then the door opened. I was expecting a blonde beauty, but there was this bloke standing there. He was mean-looking. He had sunglasses on even though it was dark. I swallowed and asked him if the girl was there. I didn't know what her name was. He laughed, and said *You're too late, Buster. We're getting hitched next week.* And then he slammed the door in my face. I stood there for five minutes, and then went home."

Jasper goes quiet again.

"That was the last time you saw her?" says Zack.

"Pretty much," he says. "Sure enough, a week later she moved out. I suppose my parents would have known her name. I mean it's possible they might still remember her. There aren't a lot of people round here who are young and pretty…"

"Aside from you," says Zack.

We hear the sound of a car pulling up outside.

"You should probably go," says Jasper.

"You embarrassed about us?" says Zack.

"On the contrary," says Jasper. "You can stay if you want, and you can ask them about the girl at forty-eight B yourself." He pushes back the chair and stands up, and looks out the window.

Zack stands up and follows his gaze. His face creases into a grimace, which means I have to look. Outside on the street is a police car. The door swings open, and out steps an even-larger version of Jasper in a policeman's uniform.

It crosses my mind that he might just have come back from a fancy dress party, but I think the chances are slim on a Sunday morning.

"You can go out by the side door," says Jasper. "Look. I'll ask my dad." He ushers us back into the kitchen and down some steps that look like they lead to a double garage.

"I bet he'll know pretty much everything about the woman at forty-eight B."

Zack is right in front of me when he stops suddenly at the bottom of the steps. I slam into his back.

I shake my head to get my bearings and peer over his shoulder.

Parked at one end of the garage is a blue Volvo, but sitting right in front of it, in iridescent red and sparkling chrome, is a five-piece premier drum kit.

Zack looks from the drums to Jasper, then back to the drums. "They your mum's?" he says.

"Yeah. Right," says Jasper. "You want to hear them?"

"Sure," I say.

"If you've got time," says Zack.

Jasper leans past us and pokes his head back through the door to the kitchen. "Be back in a minute, Dad," he yells.

He marches over to the drums, pulls back the stool, clicks on the snare, and takes two sticks from a little bag. He places the sticks together on the snare drum, shuts his eyes, draws in a long breath, and erupts into activity. He's a pulsing robot. Rolls, trills, cymbal crashes, the hi-hat, he moves around the kit like he's been playing since he was four.

"Tight," I say when he stops.

"Sweet," says Zack.

"Tight and sweet," I say.

"Thanks," says Jasper. He pulls out a handkerchief and wipes his forehead.

"You know we play in a band," says Zack.

"And we don't have a drummer," I say. "We really need one."

Jasper gives me a broad grin. "If I had more time," he says.

"You're already in a band?" I say.

"Yup," says Jasper. "We're playing in Port Jackson on Monday night. Why don't you come along?"

"Oh," says Zack. "Be really nice, but we're playing on Monday night as well."

"Wait a minute," I say, with more than a touch of trepidation. "What's the name of your band?"

"The Disappointed Parents," says Jasper.

"That makes no sense," says Zack. He stabs a finger at Jasper. "If you're in the Disappointed Parents, then how come we didn't know about it?"

"I only joined them a couple of weeks ago," says Jasper. "Their old drummer quit."

"Wow," I say. "You landed on your feet."

"I hope you're washing them on a regular basis," says Zack.

I shove myself in front of Zack. "We're the opening act," I say. "The Sand Tigers."

"The Nowhere Men," says Zack, resting his chin on my shoulder.

Jasper stands up and leads us over to the door, which is behind the Volvo. "I'll give you a ring and let you know what I find out," he says.

As we reach the pavement, Zack says, "I suppose you won."

"I won what?" I say as we march toward Norfolk Square.

"You won the bet," says Zack. "We made progress. I think we've found Julie McGuire." He spreads his arms. "You get to choose the name of the band."

"The Nowhere Men," I say. "No doubt about it."

"I thought you wanted to call us the Sand Tigers," says Zack.

"I was just testing you," I say. "I wanted to see how much you wanted the Nowhere Men. It's obviously the better name."

"Sometimes," says Zack as we reach Norfolk Square, "you can be quite annoying."

23
MONDAY

Horoscope: April 19, Aquarius:

Never the one to shy away from hard work, you will have to open up today, and allow yourself to fully experience the sunny dispositions of those around you. With that done, you will soon be able to see the generosity of spirit within yourself.

"Dressing room is not too bad." Zack screws his face up, then plinks through the guitar riff from the Beatles's "Ticket To Ride," our opening number. "As long as you inhale through your mouth."

"What's that?" I can barely hear him over the din of heavy metal, which is pounding down from the auditorium upstairs.

"I said it's a nice dressing room if you breathe through your mouth." Zack adjusts his guitar strap.

"Could do with somewhere to sit down," I yell back,

"after playing rugby and then hauling amps up and down stairs for Harry." I swivel my p-bass so it's upright, then rest the middle of my forehead against its smooth, cool neck. "So much for the free ride to the gig."

"Well, there's plenty of floor available." Zack's fingers dance up and down the fret board of his guitar.

"Fantastic," I say. "After you."

"It's a nice floor," says Zack.

"It's a bloody toilet," I say. "I'm not sitting on a toilet floor."

"Oh, come on, Toby," says Zack. "Don't be such a baby. You heard what Harry said. It's been out of use for more than a year." He bobs and dances as he hammers away at his guitar, as if he's trying to play through the entire thirty-minute set in thirty seconds. "Plus, it's the ladies'. I mean it's not like it's the gents'. That really would be disgusting."

"I don't even feel good about standing up on this floor." My legs ache so much that I lean back against a cubicle door as I attempt to tune my bass. "Look. You can almost see the bacteria wriggling out from the gaps between the tiles. Some of them are bound to get stuck to my shoes, and then they'll come home with me. Then they'll wait for me to get undressed, and then they'll pounce."

The coolness of the door actually feels quite nice through the fabric of my shirt in spite of the fact that armies of bubonic plague germs are now crawling across my shoulder.

The reason I'm only trying to tune my bass and not really succeeding is due to the din pounding down from the ceiling. The crashing guitar chords come from the main act of the evening, the Disappointed Parents, who are upstairs doing their sound check right now.

Then, with one apocalyptic eruption, the sound from upstairs ends.

We both look up at the ceiling.

"That's it," says Zack, not sounding quite so confident. "Sound check over. We go on in fifteen minutes."

"You ready?" I say.

"According to Harry," says Zack, "we have to do one very important thing." He places his guitar back in its case. "PGP. You can't go on without it."

"PGP?" I say.

"Pre-gig-piss," says Zack. "I have to run and use the toilet upstairs." He points at his guitar. "You don't need me here to tune up, do you?"

"I'm confused," I say. "Why do you have to go upstairs? You were the one who was just telling me that it's okay to sit on the floor. How come you can't use the facilities down here?"

"We're not allowed to use it," says Zack. "Rules of the management. Anyway, it's out of order." He walks over to the door and pulls it open. "Aside from anything, it's the ladies'."

"Don't get lost," I tell him. I stop leaning on the cubicle door, and take a glance inside.

It's one of those antique toilets with the cistern up by the ceiling and a chain dangling down, but it looks to be in perfect working order. I guess Zack just needed to go in search of himself for a few moments. Without taking my bass off, I negotiate my way into the cubicle and use the facilities.

When I'm done I pull the chain. It all works perfectly, and as I watch the clean water flood back in from the cistern I get a little glow. Peeing with my bass on, I actually feel like a rock star for the first time. But the nice feeling just makes my legs even more tired.

What the heck. I fasten my jeans back up, turn myself around, and slump back on the rim of the bowl. I let out a long breath as the blood trickles back into my calf muscles. It's so comfortable that I lean back against the concrete wall.

I contemplate the porcelain handle of the chain swinging in front of my face, and just let my eyes close for a moment.

24
MONDAY

But I don't have long to enjoy the feeling. There's a squeak as the outer door swings open, and footsteps echo across the floor.

"It's out of order," I say, thinking this is a woman who's ignored the sign on the door. With the long neck of the bass I have to back out of the cubicle, and as I do I come face-to-face, not with a woman, but with Pork-pie, still in his hat and sunglasses.

"Ha," I say. I feel I need to explain what I'm doing here. "Yeah, I know it's the ladies', but I figured that as it was out of order it would be okay to use it."

"Hey, my brother." He shifts his hat back on his head, revealing a pink, lined forehead. "I have no problem with that. No problem at all. You gotta go where you gotta go."

"This is actually the dressing room for both bands," I tell him. "It's kind of private."

"Oh, no problem. I hear you loud and clear." He shifts his hat forward. "You need your space. It's like a little oasis of coolness before the sandstorm up there." He points at the ceiling. "I will leave you to do, or not do, whatever it is you need to do, or not do."

He takes a couple of steps back toward the door.

"Thanks for coming, anyway," I say. "I hope you enjoy the music." I wave toward the door as a kind of hint.

He does a 180 and looks at the ceiling. "I always enjoy live music. In fact, I'm an aficionado of all of the arts. Once upon a time, I was an architecture student." He looks straight at me. "That was why I came in here. I love these old places. I like the way they were put together." He points at my bass. "Now that is a classic piece of design. The Fender precision bass. Never changed in sixty years. It's a nice instrument."

"Thanks," I say. I take a long breath. Okay. Big-decision time. "I saw you in Harry Haller's a couple of days ago."

Finally, he pulls off his glasses. At least he slides them part of the way down his nose but not so far that I can see his eyes. "Harry Haller? I'm blanking out. I have so many friends it's hard to keep track of all of them."

"Harry Haller's is a music shop," I say. "They sell instruments. You were in there looking for a p-bass."

"I love, love, love p-basses." He replaces his glasses and reaches out a bony hand. "Do you think I could take a look at that one? It looks old. You must know the pedigree and that kind of thing, like who owned it and when it was made."

"Sure. Give it a whirl." I unhook the bass from its strap and hand it to him.

He takes it left-handed again. He pulls at a string with his thumb. It makes a horrible metallic twang. I immediately regret giving it to him. He's going to put it right out of tune.

"I'd better take it back," I say, holding out my hand. "We go on in a couple of minutes."

He looks up at me, but doesn't make any move to give it back. "I want to buy this instrument from you," he says. "You mind if I just take it upstairs? The light is better, and I want to take a closer look at it."

"It's not really for sale," I say, "and in any case, it belongs to my brother. I don't exactly know how much it's worth. I mean it could be worth five hundred, or it could be worth five-thousand." I point at him. "Why don't you take your sunglasses off if you want to see it better?"

"I have the money. Cash," he says. "Right now. I could give you five thousand pounds right here, right now. Think about it. You could buy yourself half a dozen basses every bit as good as this one, plus you could equip your whole band."

"But we're just about to go on stage," I say. "What am I supposed to play?"

"The other band," he says. "Borrow their bass."

I shake my head. "Nah. I don't think that would work."

He takes a couple more steps toward the door. "Just give me one minute, good sir."

Good sir?

I think that if I live long enough, I'm going to have a family motto. I wonder what Slow on the Uptake is in Latin.

"No." I grab the instrument on a strong point around the neck, near the body. "No, Rupert."

I pull the bass back toward me, and with it comes Pork-pie. He brings his face right up to mine. So close that I can see the flecks of gray on his unshaven chin, and smell his cheesy breath.

We stay like that for a few moments, then he hisses, "Yes, Rupert." He flips the bass over, jerking it out of my grip, then swings it back and levels it at my face as if he's about to hit me with it.

"Peek-a-Boo." The door swings open behind Rupert, and Jasper pokes his head around it. "Anyone home?" he says.

Rupert twists around as Jasper clomps into the room and stands in front of the doorway, which he blocks quite easily.

"Can't you read, mate?" he says to Rupert. "The sign on the door says that this room is closed, so scram, my friend."

"It's cool, it's cool." Rupert bobs his head. "I was just

having a heart-to-heart with my good buddy here." As he says this, he moves toward the door still holding the bass. "If you would let me through."

"No! Wait," I say, and I say it more to Jasper than to Rupert. "You can't take the bass. I need it."

Pork-pie grins at Jasper. "This kid is paranoid. I have no idea what he thinks I'm going to do with his bass."

Jasper moves to one side, giving Rupert room to leave.

"No," I say. "That's my bass. Don't let him take it."

Jasper puts one hand on Rupert's shoulder. "Sorry, Buster," he says. "I'm not sure I have any idea where you're going with that bass either." With swift moves, he relieves Rupert of the bass and shoves him out through the door.

Rupert stumbles into the corridor, but almost immediately finds his footing. He turns to face us, looking first at me, then at Jasper. "That was uncalled for, my friends." He straightens his jacket. "To be continued," he says.

Jasper closes the door without even looking at Rupert. "How do you feel?" he says, and hands me back my bass.

"Ready as I'll ever be," I say, and I actually hug the bass.

Jasper laughs. "I wouldn't leave it unattended if I were you."

"Yeah. You're probably right," I say. "Thanks for helping me out there. For a minute I thought I'd lost my bass."

"I thought you knew him," says Jasper.

"No. I've never seen him before," I say. "Well, I have seen him, but I don't know who he is."

"Well, he finagled his way in without paying," says

Jasper. "He said he was a friend of the band. None of us knew who he was so we figured he knew you."

"He says he wants to buy my bass, and he has the money on him," I say. "I think he was just a bit impatient."

"Well, he must be the stingiest guy on the planet, because he not only refused to pay to get in, but he also scrounged a free drink at the bar." Jasper gives a short laugh, and then looks serious. "I actually came down here to let you know that I found out where that Julie McGuire lives," he says. "You want me to give you the details now?"

He doesn't get a chance to finish, as there's another knock on the door.

"It's the bloody ladies' room," shouts Jasper.

This time the door opens all the way, and Zack steps in. "Ladies?" he says to Jasper, then he looks right at me. "I don't think so."

Harry appears behind Zack. "Please come," he says. "Your destiny is waiting for you, my friends."

"Thanks," I say to Jasper. "Can we talk about this later?" I bash the neck of my bass against the edge of the narrow doorway as I try to steer through it.

"Maybe I should ring you tomorrow," he says.

"Good idea." I swing the neck upright so I don't bang it on anything else, then I follow Harry out of the toilet, into a pitch-black corridor, and up the steps.

25
MONDAY

Harry pulls the door all the way open. "Go, go, GO!!" he yells, like he's a sky-diving instructor kicking his students out of the plane.

Zack crosses himself, wipes his sweaty hands on his jeans, then turns to me and shouts, "Yeah! Come on! Let's do it! Let's knock 'em dead," as if everything is still okay. As if this is just the first of many gigs.

Zack leaps out onto the stage, and I'm just about to follow him when I feel a hand grip my shoulder.

Rupert! I think, and ice shoots through my limbs, but when I spin around to confront him I find myself face-to-face with a scowling Harry. He pokes each of his index fingers into the corners of his sad mouth, and pushes them up so it looks like he's smiling.

I stretch my own mouth into a grin.

Harry twists his mouth into a lopsided smile and shrugs, then nods.

I give him a thumbs-up, then turn and chase after Zack, keeping my eyes glued to the soggy orange carpet that covers the stage.

This would not be a good time to trip over any of the cables that snake between the main act's amplifiers, speaker cabinets, drums, guitar stands, keyboards, and microphones.

Staring at the carpet also means I don't have to look at the audience. There's no cheering, no applause, no disembodied voice announcing, *Ladies and Gentlemen, allow me to introduce the fantastic new sensation from Port Jackson! The Nowhere Men!* in a hurried baritone.

The disco music fades out to nothing and there's silence, but as my ears get accustomed to the quietness there are more sounds within it. There's a clink of glasses, and the sound of someone crumpling a crisp bag.

A couple of people clap—Zack's friends probably— and somebody calls out "Zack, my man!"

Ordinary sounds.

I would prefer silence. Silence is kind of special. Silence would mean everyone has stopped what they're doing to watch us. Ordinary sounds mean that everyone's gone back to whatever it was they were doing before we went on stage.

I see our mic stands over on the left-hand side of the stage. They're sitting in their own beam of dusty light in a narrow ledge between a speaker cabinet the size of a wardrobe, and the edge of the stage itself.

Cradling the bass so I don't knock it against anything, I insert myself into my little patch of carpet. It's just wide enough for me to stand upright with my feet apart. I slide the bass down into playing position and turn to confront the audience.

Zack slides in next to me, then turns sideways so there's room for both of us. For the last six weeks we've been rehearsing in a tiny bedroom, barely bigger than a broom closet. But even in that broom closet we've never had to play standing this close together.

So this is it. This is really it.

With a massive effort I force my chin up so I'm facing the audience, and then stretch my mouth into my best fake grin.

The fake grin that tells the audience that I'm not the least bit scared to be standing up here, even though I am.

The fake grin that tells the audience that I know all the songs backward, which I'm not sure I do.

The fake grin that tells the audience that this is the first of many gigs, as opposed to the first and last gig.

Hopefully with the hazy lighting and the distance between me and them, the grimace will pass as a grin.

Yup. There really are only twelve of them. But at least there's nobody wearing a pork pie hat.

A mere dozen people in the entire history of the universe will hear the Nowhere Men perform live, and that includes the bloke behind the table selling Coke and crisps. For one second I think there might be another figure, lurking in the shadows, but I'd rather have twelve in the audience than thirteen. Although it would be poetic if Rupert was the thirteenth.

Maybe it's just as well there won't be many witnesses, but I wish somebody was here to take a picture. Something to show my grandchildren. I frame the view, then blink my eyes as if I'm taking a photo. As if I can put this picture in the back of my mind and keep it forever.

I find the power cable. There's a loud buzz and hum as I stick the jack plug into the amp. Zack turns his back to the audience and twangs a low E for tuning. When he turns back he whacks the head of his guitar against the body of my bass, creating a humungous boom, which then reverberates around the room.

It's the loudest noise I've ever made, but oddly enough it's in tune. It's probably the loudest noise Shawn's bass has ever made.

I shuffle sideways so the mic is right in front of my mouth. It's actually just a fraction high for me, but it's too late to adjust it now. Anyway, it'll force me to keep my head up while I sing.

"Hello," I say into the little serrated, metal ball of

the mic. I've realized I can't make myself sound like I'm a native of Port Jackson, but I try to make myself sound as non-London as possible. My voice echoes back from the auditorium. "Hello, Day Trippers," I say, the last *S* echoing off windows, pillars, wallpaper, and the twelve members of the audience who are shuffling around to face us like a group of zombies who've just got a whiff of live brains. "This is your ticket to ride."

A couple of them even clap again.

I step back from the mic and arrange my fingers on the bass strings, then blank out.

What is this instrument?

How do I play it?

Who am I?

Then it comes back to me. "One, two, three—" and we both hit the first note like a bulls-eye, the second note follows it, then the third, and our first and last gig has begun. It's as unstoppable as a boulder tumbling down a hill.

I stretch up to the mic. "I think I'm going to be sad," I croon, in perfect harmony with Zack, and almost immediately my brain starts to play tricks on me.

The bad news is that there really is a thirteenth person in the audience, leaning on a pillar in the shadows. The good news is that she's not wearing a pork pie hat. She's probably just some friend of the other band, but just because she's a girl of about five-foot nothing, with long dark hair, my brain has to turn her into Michelle.

Of course, I know it's not her. It's just my mind playing tricks. But just as it happened at the Brunswick Bus Station, even though I know that this isn't Michelle, I can't take my eyes off her until I'm absolutely certain.

Keeping to the shadows, the Girl-Who-Isn't-Michelle shuffles forward to one of the empty seats just in front of me. She slumps into it, her chin tucked down into her collarbones and her hands shoved into her armpits.

Typical. If my brain is going to pretend that Michelle's here, then why can't it invent a Michelle who's happy to see me?

Yup. The magic of the moment of my first time on stage is over. I really do think that I'm going to be sad, and more likely than not it's going to be today-yay, but probably for very different reasons than the ones Lennon and McCartney wrote about in their song.

26
MONDAY

They say that you never forget your first gig, and I'm sure that's going to turn out to be true, but for me the moment that will probably be imprinted on my mind like a permanent tattoo is the time when the first song ends.

We hit the last chord of "Ticket to Ride." The notes reverberate around the auditorium, and echo away into silence like the ripples when you throw a rock into a pond.

Somebody coughs, and a car passes outside with its stereo blasting. I raise my hand to hit the first note of "Can't Buy Me Love," but my fingers are numb. I can't play the note.

Didn't even one single person like us?

Can't one person clap?

I glance over at the Girl-Who-Isn't-Michelle. *You're no help,* I think. Great. Now I can't even make figments of my imagination clap.

And then the strangest thing happens. Bogus Michelle stands up, walks toward the stage, and steps into the edge of the lights.

"Yay!" she yells, and pounds her hands together.

Bloody heck. It's not the Girl-Who-Isn't-Michelle. It's real Michelle. Of all people. This still makes no sense. All this time I'd been assuming that she didn't like me. Maybe even hated me. But if that's the case, then why is she clapping for us?

The next thing that happens is that someone else begins to clap. At first I think it's a derisory slow hand clap, but it speeds up, and then there's whistling. Then more clapping.

A tingle runs up my legs, up my spine, and makes the back of my neck burn. This is it. A heavyset kid comes and stands next to Michelle. She only comes up to his elbow. He's joined by another. I think they're friends of Zack.

Soon we have half a dozen fans right in front of the stage.

Something moves in the corner of my eye. Harry is still standing in the stage doorway. He's making a rotating gesture with his arm. I know exactly what he means. Start the next song before the applause dies down.

I nod to Zack and he hammers out the guitar intro to "Can't Buy Me Love."

After that it seems like we play for the next twenty-seven minutes without stopping for even a second, and the twenty-seven minutes hurtle past us like twenty-seven seconds. Each song is note perfect. The sound balance is good. Zack's guitar is just loud enough that you can hear his solos and fills, but not so loud that he drowns out the vocals.

Finally, Zack strikes the ending chord of our last song, "Get Back." This time we don't hear the notes echo; the applause is even louder than the music. Of course, the audience is bigger by the time we finish, as about forty of the Disappointed Parents's crowd has been filtering in while we're playing, and they seem to like us too.

Do I feel like a rock star? For thirty minutes that feel more like thirty seconds, I do. It's amazing. It's stupendous. Somebody once said we all get fifteen minutes of fame, but who would have guessed that the fifteen minutes would only feel like fifteen seconds. Still, fifteen seconds is better than nothing.

Not only is the crowd applauding, but they're shouting for more and yelling out requests. Harry signals for us to get off the stage. I'm nearest the door. I unplug the guitar lead and head straight over, but just as we get to the door the chanting begins.

More! More!

Zack places his hand on my shoulder, and yells something at me.

"What?" I say. I stop opening the door.

"We could do 'Back in the USSR,'" he says.

I take a step back out of the doorway, but Harry grabs my shoulder.

"They want us to keep playing," I say. "We should do another one."

Harry shakes his head. He puts his hand on my back and, gently but firmly, guides me through the stage doorway and closes the door behind the three of us.

"What's the matter?" says Zack. "Didn't you like us?"

Harry shakes his head. "You were excellent. Almost too good." The sound of the clapping and cheers are muffled by the closed door, and then peter out after a few seconds. "You could be a tough act to follow."

"Why couldn't we do one more?" says Zack. "Sounds like they want us to." Zack points back to the stage door. "I mean you're not going on for half an hour or so, and we're better than the disco."

"First rule of show business." Harry presses his hands together. "Leave your fans wanting more. Not to mention," he laughs, "we need most of that half hour to move our equipment into the right position to play." He folds his arms across his chest. "On a happier note, we have three gigs a week for the next six months," he says. "If you can, I would like you to play support for all of them, and I will pay you fifty pounds a throw."

Zack bites his lower lip, and shakes his head.

"What's up?" says Harry, frowning. "I thought you'd be over the moon."

I pull my fake grin. "No. It's fine. It's great news," I say.

I look at Zack. "Really good," he says.

"We'll talk about the details tomorrow." Harry steps back out onto the stage.

"Bummer," says Zack, after Harry closes the door.

"You don't have to tell me." I point toward the stage door with the headstock of the bass. "Listen, there's someone out there I want to see." I stumble back down the stairs to the toilet-dressing-room.

"It's Harry I'm not looking forward to telling," says Zack, following me.

Midway down the staircase, we run into the remainder of the Disappointed Parents coming up the other way.

"Nice one!" they yell.

They slap our backs as we squeeze past, which would be more fun if I wasn't so sweaty.

"Break a leg," I shout back at them.

"Thanks, mates," Jasper yells back, then they head up to the top of the stairs.

"It's a hundred fifty a week," says Zack.

"Blame Shawn," I say. "Not me."

Back in the dressing room, we throw our guitars into their cases, then I hurtle back up the stairs again. Once again, I have to squeeze past the Disappointed Parents at the top of the stairs.

"You look like a man on a mission," says Jasper.

I march out across the stage, and jump down into the audience.

But she's gone. She's not there.

Another hand slaps against my back, pushing my shirt against icy sweat.

"Good one, mate," says somebody else.

Another hand slaps me on the shoulder, then another. I turn and grin at faces I've never seen before. "Thanks. Thanks."

"Loved it, man!"

"Thanks." I stumble backward and another hand grips my shoulder. I turn around and look into the face of the guy who was actually standing beside Michelle. "You know the short girl you were standing next to?"

"Are you talking about the girl in the blue sweater?" he says.

"Right," I say. "Did you see where she went?"

"Very nice." The guy makes an exaggerated wink. "What's it worth?"

"Aw c'mon, man!" I say.

The guy takes a step back. "It's okay. I was just ragging you." He laughs. "The moment you stopped playing, I asked her name. She looked at me like I'd trodden on her foot, and then made a bolt for the exit. You have my sincerest sympathies."

I run to the exit. I look up and down the row of cars parked outside, but there's nobody.

I retrace my steps back to the dressing room. Nothing

makes sense. Why did she come to the gig if she didn't want to have anything to do with me? I take my bass out again and this time I wipe down the strings so they don't rust. I wish I'd brought a dry shirt to change into.

If she went to all the trouble to come over here, then why didn't she stay to at least say hello?

Did she come to see Zack? He doesn't even know her.

There's a rap on the door and Harry comes in. "If you are ready to leave right away I'll give you a lift home," he says. "But we have to go right now. I have to return in twenty minutes in order to go onstage myself."

"I'm ready." I pull my sweater over my head and pick up Shawn's bass. "Let's go."

"I'm going to hang around," says Zack. "I might as well take in the Disappointed Parents while I'm here."

"Very gentlemanly of you," says Harry.

Now I feel like a rat. I should have stayed to hear Harry, but I don't feel up for it. I have a lot on my mind.

I follow Harry out of the dressing room, down the hall, and out into the street where his transit van is idling by the curb. He pulls open one of the back doors.

"My first ride in a gig bus," I say. "Now I feel like a real rock star."

"I regret to tell you that the glamour will probably fade fast," says Harry. "I hope you don't mind riding in the back," he says. "I have a great deal of equipment in the cab."

"That's fine," I say. I slide the bass case onto the floor of the van, then climb in after it.

"Oh, and please mind where you step, Toby," says Harry. "You will be sharing with another passenger."

"What?" I say. I spin around, just in time to see the door slam behind me. It's pitch black. "Hello," I say, to whomever it is.

"Hi," says a girl's voice. A very familiar voice.

"Michelle!"

27
MONDAY

The van's motor revs and I'm thrown backward. Presumably this is what Harry meant by the glamour fading fast. I shuffle my feet to try to find balance, but then a small hand fastens around my wrist, and pulls me down onto the wheel-arch next to her. I feel Michelle's warm shoulder against mine, and I smell her chai tea smell.

"What?" I begin to say, but a hand closes over my mouth.

"I'm right up shit creek," she says. "Harry's taking me to the bus station. We have about two minutes. Mum's going to murder me when I get back."

We lurch over to the left, and the van creaks and groans as if it's about to fall apart. I flail my free hand, and my fingertips hook onto a ridge jutting out of the wall of the van. This time it's me who pulls us back onto the wheel-arch.

"Thanks," says Michelle. "I just wanted to see you, and tell you I was sorry. Turns out my mom saw us walking back from the park. I was back in Brunswick about forty-five minutes after I left you. I never thought of Brunswick as jail before."

We're thrown forward, and then backward. I keep my fingers hooked into the metal ridge.

"Can you come over to Brunswick sometime?" she says. "I'd still really like to have that second cup of tea with you."

"Oh, man," I say. "Why do things always have to work out like this?" We're both thrown upward as the van hits a bump. "My whole life has turned upside down in the last couple of days. Nothing related to what happened to you. Or even what happened between us. Listen, we only have a couple of minutes, but the worst of it is that I have to go back to London."

"Going to London doesn't sound too awful," she says. "How long are you going for?"

"For good," I say, as a car blasts its horn behind us.

"You mean you aren't coming back?" She squeezes my hand harder.

"Well, maybe on holiday once in a while, but, no. Not really." I twist my hand around and interlock it with her fingers. "I don't suppose I'll be heading back here in the near future."

"Why? You have the band. It was amazing," she says. "You have to stay. Why would you want to go back now?"

We lurch forward as the van brakes, then we're thrown backward. "I don't want to go back," I say. "Sure. I'd like to go back there for a holiday, but to stay? No. No way. This is my home now."

"Can't you stay here somehow?" says Michelle.

"It's my mom," I say. "She has to go back. Obviously, I have to go with her."

A siren wails past.

"Unless your dad wants to adopt me."

"You probably wouldn't be his first choice," she says.

"Things are all messed up here for us," I say. "I don't have time to tell you everything."

I'm thrown over to the left as the van swerves to the right. I'm beginning to feel like I'm doing one of those zero-gravity exercises that astronauts have to go through. I swing my hand up, and manage to grab onto a metal spar as I fly past, then lower myself next to Michelle again.

The van squeals to a halt, and Harry comes around to open the door. "First stop, Port Jackson bus station."

"Bye," says Michelle. She leans forward and kisses me on the cheek. As she stands up she thrusts something into my hand. I shove it into my pocket without looking at it.

I stand up with her. I want to kiss her back, but everything happened so fast. I have just a glimpse of her as she runs toward the bus platforms, and then the door is closed and I'm back in the dark again. I feel my way back to the wheel-arch, and I have just enough time to brace myself before Harry roars off again. It's a lot easier hanging on to the spar on my own, but I would give anything to have Michelle clutching my hand again.

Without Michelle, I don't want to be in here. I slide toward the front of the van, and hammer on the dividing wall just behind where I reckon Harry's head is. I'm thrown forward as the van jerks to a halt once again.

I listen to the driver's door slam, footsteps, and then the back doors swing open. "Are you okay?" says Harry.

"I want to walk from here," I say.

"It's not really a great place to walk from," he says. "I'm going right past your house."

"I just want to decompress after the gig. I feel all wound up."

I grab my bass and hustle out onto wet asphalt. "You know where you are?" asks Harry.

Behind me is the harbor. A big tanker is all lit up. I used to like going and looking at ships. Maybe I'll go and take a look and dream about working my way back here from London on a coal barge. In front of me are some down-and-out hotels, and off to the left is the ocean, with its waves breathing softly.

"Yup." I nod. "I know where I am."

"Do not dawdle," says Harry as he jumps back into the

cab and slams the door behind him. "Go straight home, okay?"

"Promise," I say. I step back onto the curb, and watch while the van pulls away. As the tail lights fade, the night wraps itself around me. A breath of wind reminds me of the sweat that hasn't dried on my back, and I unfold the note Michelle gave me. Her name, address in Brunswick, her phone number, and the words *Please ring me between four and six.*

I take out the Julie McGuire message. I fold Michelle's note up with them and put it all back in my pocket.

I stare at the empty street trying to figure out what to do next. Finally, a car swishes past on the wet asphalt.

28
MONDAY

Ocean Road is wide here. Six lanes. The truth of the matter is that I don't really want to go home just yet. There's nothing there for me apart from Mom trying to work out how we can survive another week. After the car passes, everything goes silent apart from the sound of waves breaking on the beach behind me, and I realize how sore my legs are.

It's nine-thirty. Apart from a brief sit-down in the van, between the rugby match, the roadie-ing, and the gig, I've been on my feet constantly for about seven hours. There are benches on the promenade. It's not a cold night, and it might be good to take a break for half an hour before slogging home.

Be nice to take a look at the briny, anyway, but the problem is how to get there. Between me and the promenade is a steep bushy slope that drops about twenty feet down to a little park. Alternatively, there's a nice concrete walkway about a hundred yards ahead.

The idea of scrambling down a slope makes my tired feet ache even more. I'm about to make my way to the path when I notice that the car that just passed me has stopped about a hundred yards up the street. My heart sinks. It's an ancient, black Honda. It does a U-turn; with its tires squealing, it heads back toward where I'm standing.

Before I can even think about running, the Civic stops directly opposite me on the other side of the road.

The door opens and Rupert steps out. He looks up and down Marine Drive, then at me. "Hey, Mister Bassman," he says. "That was a very memorable musical event, if I may say so." He slams the car door shut. "You look like a man who's in need of a lift home."

I shake my head.

"I insist. I think it's time we took a little drive in my car." He saunters slowly across the wide street with his hands still in his pockets, his shaggy hair whipping in the breeze. In spite of the cold he has his shirt sleeves rolled up, exposing the rope-like tendons in his forearms.

"I'm okay actually," I say. A shiver runs through me.

"I'm pretty wound up after the gig, and I wanted to walk home to relax a little."

"Here. I get the feeling it's been a long day for you, good sir." He takes one hand out of his pocket and holds it out toward me. "Let me take that for you." He points to the bass. "I can see that it's been such a heavy burden. There's really no need for you to carry it anymore."

"No." I say. "Rupert." I swallow to get rid of the dryness in my mouth. "It's not yours." I swing the case behind my back and, at least for a moment, out of his reach.

"No, Rupert," he says in a squeaky voice. "Please don't steal my bass." He reaches into his back pocket, and whips out a long metal object.

Some kind of tool.

He flicks a switch with his thumb, and the blade slides out.

It's a Stanley knife.

He holds the knife up at eye level, presumably just in case I hadn't noticed it already. "It's not your bass either, my friend." He steps forward and lunges at my face with the blade. "I know that, and you know that."

I glance one way along Marine Parade, and then the other. I don't know what I'm looking for. Maybe someone to rescue me. But there's not a soul in sight.

"No more games." He tilts his head side to side, then slashes at me with the blade again. "Give me the bass."

Something snaps in my head. I hug the case to my chest, spin around, and leap into the dark undergrowth behind me. The ground drops away under my feet, and I stumble and slither into deeper and deeper darkness. Sharp branches snap and crack against the hard surface of the case. It's desperate. It's probably stupid, but it's all I can do.

"You don't want to go down there, good sir." The voice above me now. "Very nasty!"

Finally, I come to a full stop on level ground. It's pitch black. I could just stay here. He'll get bored and leave.

No.

Sticks are breaking above me. One snap, and then another. He can't see me, but he's trailing me. I must have cut a path through the bushes that a blind man could follow. Then I see a slither of bright orange. Crap! He has a flashlight. No. It's flickering orange. It's a match or a cigarette lighter.

The sounds of snapping branches get closer. Fear wins out. I know that I've always said that the only luck I have is bad luck, but right now I have to hope for good luck. I take the thin bass case and prop it against the shrub I'm next to. It's black, and it won't move, and there's a chance that he won't be able to find it with the cigarette lighter, and even if he does, maybe he'll be happy to get the bass, and he'll leave me alone.

Hell! No way is he getting the bass. I lift it and wedge it high into the upper branches of the shrub. When it's up as far as it'll go, I force it farther. He'll need more than a cigarette lighter to find it now.

Wedging the bass into the shrub is a far-from-silent process, and he hears me right away.

"I'm right here, my friend," he chants. "Just reach out and I'll be there."

In your dreams, Buster. I crash through the bushes sideways, pulling at branches as I go to make as much noise as possible. In a few seconds I'm twenty or thirty paces away from where I hid the bass.

"There's no business like show business." Rupert's voice drifts out of the pitch-darkness. "And there's no show like a no-show." The sound of snapping branches pauses for a moment, then it begins to move away from both me and where I put the bass. "Where are you, my good sir? We need to have a chat."

Fantastic. That part of the plan worked; now all I have to do is save my own skin.

I turn at right angles, and head straight toward the sea. Three paces and I'm out in the open. After running through the bushes, my shirt is full of things that scratch and prickle. When I'm out in the open, the breeze chills right through me.

"It's the Port Jackson mini-marathon," he cries.

The ground rises a little, and running footsteps pound behind me. I plunge back into a second row of bushes only a couple feet wide. On the other side of the bushes is a row of beach huts. There's just enough room for me to squeeze myself into the gap between two of them. Now I'm back out on the promenade by a closed-down cafeteria. A yellow street lamp buzzes and casts a pool of light ahead of me. I hear sounds of more branches breaking behind me.

I take a deep breath and sprint across the pool of light.

"It's the triathlon!" cries Rupert.

I vault over the waist-high handrail and crash down onto the pebbles. It's actually a much deeper drop than I expected. I sprawl onto my back when I hit the ground, but I roll straight back up to my feet, and then I freeze.

A voice above me. "Come, my good sir. Let's stop this silliness!" Still close. Too close.

The promenade above me casts a deep shadow. Still, I can't stay here. He can't see me for now, but if he comes down to the beach he'll use his lighter again, and he won't have much trouble finding me.

He can probably see in the dark anyway.

I can't stay, but I can't move either. I'm surrounded by pebbles. If I make even the slightest movement, the rocks will crunch, and he will know exactly where I am.

I study the little waves sloshing up onto the rocks.

A triathlon, he said.

Is there any chance whatsoever that Rupert can't swim?

Probably not, but it's the only hope I've got.

The waves are only ten yards in front of me, but ten yards is still a long way, especially over rocks.

Oh well. If I'm going to be stupid, I might as well be totally stupid.

I reach down and grab a handful of small rocks. It's a

trick that's worked in a thousand bad films. Probably no chance of working in real life.

I hurl the rocks as far as I can over to the left.

Without waiting to see if the falling rocks sound anything at all like footsteps on a different part of the beach, I sprint down to the water's edge, tug my shoes off my feet, and run into the waves. For a moment, I don't feel the cold, but then iciness crawls up my shin bones.

Footsteps crunch on the pebbles right behind me. "Come on, good sir. It's too late for the triathlon."

I take another step. My foot lands on a sharp rock and I stumble forward. The beach is steep. I'm up to my waist.

"You're a crazy fellow," says a voice from behind. "Maybe even a lunatic! You'll catch your death."

I turn to see his silhouette framed against the lights on the promenade. He's at the water line.

Yup. Crazy maybe. Stupid definitely. If I can see the lights then I'm all lit up, and even if Rupert can't swim, he can still wade out and get me.

I stretch my arms over my head and plunge into the salty blackness.

I swim underwater as far as I can, then up to the surface. I keep going straight out with short, quick strokes, one, two, breathe, one, two, breathe. I roll onto my back and try to make out what's happening on the beach behind me. The neon sign of the old West End Café gives everything a red glow, and I can make out something that looks like a silhouette, but it might just be a wooden post from the old breakwater.

Am I safe?

I roll onto my stomach again. Fifty strokes. This time I windmill my shoulders. I reach forward as far as I can go, then roll, and pull my hand back to my knee.

Catch the bubbles, Toby. Catch the bubbles. Jeannette, my old swim teacher dances on the side of the pool. She once swam the ten miles across the Sound. If she could see me now, she would be so proud.

Water rushes down my shirt as I propel myself forward. Not cold. Not warm. I lose count, and then I hit a patch of water so cold it freezes my arms instantly. I roll over and doggy paddle until I get back to the warmer water.

There's not much of a swell. I just hang there and tread water. The sound of the waves breaking seems a long way off now. No sounds of anyone splashing out to apprehend me. Just distant sounds.

A car horn.

A plane overhead.

The putter of an outboard motor.

I think about Michelle's note. I hope that she wrote it in waterproof ink, then I think about how we met at the shark tank. Naturally this leads me to think about what was in the shark tank.

Were those local sharks?

What did Michelle tell me about Frosty?

That he deliberately dived with sharks?

Did he do it around here?

Panic shoots up my spine, and the next moment I'm swimming as fast as I can toward the shore.

If Rupert is still there, then God bless him. He can have the reward for his patience. If he wants the old note from Julie McGuire in my soggy pocket, then he's more than welcome to it.

I swim directly to the shore rather than back to my starting point. Mostly this is just practicality. It's a shorter swim, but it'll also give me more chance of escape in the unlikely event that he's still hanging about. I picture him standing at the spot where I dove in.

Finally, I reach my leg down and my feet touch the bottom. I swim a few more strokes then half-walk, half-stumble back onto the pebbles. My arms and legs ache with the exertion, and I just want to lie down.

The breeze catches me and chills me to the bone. I turn right and walk back to where I went in. I have no hope of finding my shoes in the dark, but then I stop below the café and turn toward the shoreline and step straight onto the shoes. They're now about twenty feet from the waves. The tide must be going out.

I jog up to the promenade.

I squeeze back between two of the huts. I scrape through the bushes. I cross the open space, which I can now see is a putting green. I reach the second row of bushes. I plunge again. I really have no explanation for this, but on the third tree I reach into, I put my hand straight on the bass case. I pull it out, unflick the latches. It's still in there.

Half an hour later I crawl into bed. Buried under extra covers, I don't stop shivering before I fall asleep.

29
TUESDAY

Horoscope: April 20, Aquarius:
You will find boundless opportunities for
exercise today. Big ideas keep drfiting by,
but you will have to wade in and catch one
if you are going to make any use of them
by the end of the day.

The next morning I wait for Mom to go to work, then I bring the wheelbarrow up from the basement. I spend ten minutes running up and down the stairs and loading it up with Shawn's bass, the amplifier, leads, mic stand, and cables. I even throw in my old classical guitar. Once I'm loaded up, I wheel down to Harry Haller's and get there just after he opens.

"It looks like you've got some really nice equipment there," he says. He puts down the accordion he's working on and comes around the counter to look into my wheelbarrow. "Some really good stuff. Are you sure you want to trade it in?"

"I'm not trading it in," I say. "I actually want to sell it."

"Okay. But if you want to upgrade to some better stuff," he says, "I will give you a better deal if you're trading than if you just want cash."

"No. I'm not going to upgrade," I say. "I'm selling it all. I'm quitting."

Harry's half smile twists into a look of dismay. "Wait a minute." He holds up his hands as if he's trying to block a punch. "What are you talking about?" he says. "I just offered you a really good deal. Between you and Zack, you can make at least seventy-five pounds a week each. That's a fortune for somebody of your age."

"Yes. I know," I say. "You made us a generous offer, but I have to sell this equipment." I have to look down at the wheelbarrow. I can't look him in the eye. "I know it sounds mad, but my mom and I have to go back to London and, basically we're broke."

"I lived in London for a while," he says. "It's a harsh place." He grins at me. "They used to call me Hairy Howler. It's an expensive place too." He does his almost-smile and says, "I can understand your need to get together as much money as you can."

He moves some music books and the accordion to one end of the counter and unloads the items one at a time. First he pulls out the coiled electrical leads. "I can't really give you anything for these," he says, as he piles them onto the counter. "I can't sell secondhand leads." He takes out the mic and the stand. "This is very nice." He points to the mic. He slides out the bass and props it against the counter, then he hauls the amp out onto the floor, and stands back to examine everything.

"I actually don't want to sell the bass," I say. "At least not just yet." I tap the case. "You said you could tell me how much it's worth."

"First things first." He slides the heavy amp against the counter. "Let's look at what you do want to sell." He points at the pile he's made in front of the counter. "The amp, the speakers, two mic stands, and two mics." He picks up one of the mics. "This is the most valuable thing aside from the bass."

He produces a notebook and pencil from his pocket, and jots some things down. I try to see what he's writing, but it seems to be in some kind of code. Or maybe it's just his handwriting. He stops writing and holds the tip of the pencil an inch above the pad. "I can give you five hundred for everything without the bass," he says.

"Five hundred?" I wasn't expecting to get a fortune, but I wasn't expecting that little. "You can't do more?"

"I wish I could." He shakes his head. "If I didn't know you, it would probably be four hundred." He walks back behind the counter, puts away his notebook, and produces a sheet of paper. "Tell you what." He pulls a pen from his inside pocket. "Advertise it on the notice board. Write a list and put prices. I'll take ten percent of whatever you sell."

He pushes the pen and paper toward me. "Even with my commission you'll make twice as much. Maybe three times."

"It'll take time though," I say.

He shakes his head. "A couple of weeks at the most."

"I don't have a couple of weeks," I say.

"That's the problem," he says. "If you need the money fast, then you're going to have to take less."

"I don't understand," I say. "If I can get a thousand for these myself, then why can't you give me more than five hundred?"

"If you advertise the equipment, then it's a private sale," he says. "If I buy it from you and sell it to someone else, then it's a business deal. I have to pay purchase tax, and VAT."

I gaze at the stuff, as if a cable or a mic stand will suddenly come to life and offer me another option.

"Okay," I say, "give me five hundred."

In just a few swift moves, Harry sweeps everything out of sight behind the counter, then writes me out a check. I ask him to make it out to Mom. Emily Holland. "Put it in your pocket right now," he says. "If you lose it we'll be in a real mess."

Next, he kneels down, opens the bass case, and takes out the instrument. "You understand," he says, "that I can give you a valuation for insurance purposes." He turns it upside down on the counter. "The figure I'll give you is theoretical. If I value it at a thousand pounds, that doesn't mean I'm going to give you a thousand pounds for it. It just means that you could sell it for a thousand pounds. If it got stolen and it was insured, then you could reasonably demand a thousand from insurance."

"Okay," I say. I smile now even though my heart is beginning to sink.

He studies the metal plate, where the neck joins the body. He jumps back, changes his glasses, and scrutinizes the number again. After that he takes out the notepad again and jots down the number. He puts the pad away and frowns at me. "How did you get this instrument?"

"It belonged to my brother," I say. Now I feel like an idiot. With a bass like this I ought to know its history. "He got it about a year and a half back. I don't know how much he paid for it or where he got it." I take a long breath.

"Okay, Toby. This is very important," he says. "You need to ask your brother where he got the bass."

"That's not going to be possible," I say.

"Wait." Harry leans forward. "Is he okay?"

"He's alive," I say, "but it's going to be hard to ask him about it." I point to the instrument. "Can't you value it just from the serial number?"

"Yes and no," says Harry. "It has a four-digit serial number, Toby," he says. "That means it's one of the first ten thousand instruments Fender made." He nods at me. "It's from the 1960s." He pats the pocket where he put his notepad. "At a rough guess it's from '67 or '68."

"So it could be worth 5,000 pounds," I say.

He puffs out his cheeks. "As I said. Yes and no." He

places his hands just above the fret board, but doesn't touch it. "It could be worth a lot more."

"I thought you told the bloke with the pork pie hat that a '60s p-bass was worth 5,000," I say.

"Yes, but there are some basses that are worth a lot more." Harry flutters his eyelids as if he doesn't quite approve of what he's going to say next. "They're called Lost Basses." He shakes his head as if it pains him to tell me this.

"I don't understand," I say.

"There's this whole obsession among collectors to find instruments that were once owned by famous musicians, but have somehow vanished." Harry patters his fingers on top of the counter. "For example, there's the bass that was owned by James Jamerson. He was the bassist who played backing on nearly every Motown hit in the 1960s. His bass was stolen just after he died." Harry claps his hands together. "It's never been seen again." He points to Shawn's instrument. "This one is not it," he says, "but it could be one of the others."

"What makes you think it's a Lost Bass?" I say.

"It's from the '60s," he says, "and they're nearly all from the sixties. Plus, and don't take this the wrong way, but they are all lost"—he makes air quotes with his fingers—"because they were all stolen."

"But my brother paid for this," I say.

"Is your brother very rich?" says Harry. "Did he have 5,000 pounds to spend on a bass? Because that is the very least this instrument could be worth."

"Five hundred," I say. "At least that's what he told me."

"So whoever sold it to him," says Harry, "did not know the value of what he was selling." Harry lifts the bass up as though it's a fragile vase, and puts it back in the case. "The reason he did not know the value is because he stole it."

"Are you going to file a police report or something?" I say.

"Good God, no." Harry closes the case and hands it to me. "I will do some research and get back to you."

"How long will that take?" I say.

"No more than a day or two." He walks over and puts a hand on my shoulder. "Toby, you have to understand that there's a lot of money to be made buying and selling old musical instruments—electric guitars and basses more than any other instruments. Where there's a lot of money changing hands, there are always a few dodgy characters. Take the bass home, and put it away carefully."

The phone is ringing just as I arrive home. I struggle in through the front door and pick up, but it's not Harry. It's Jasper with Julie McGuire's number.

30
TUESDAY

As the bus pulls into Brunswick Station, I catch sight of Michelle standing under the clock, right where we agreed to meet. According to the clock, it's four, and I should already be at Julie McGuire's. My concern for the bass is now added to my worry about being late. The last thing I want is to get to Julie's, find she's out, and have to carry the bass all the way home again.

A moment later, both bus and Michelle are out of sight as the bus turns a corner. I stand up before the bus stops, and then get thrown forward as it jerks to a halt, but I'm back on my feet in a second. With a huge sense of relief, I grab the bass and race up the aisle.

Michelle is waiting by the door.

"Oh man, I'm sorry you had to wait," I say as I step down onto the asphalt. "There was a big accident on Coast Road. We got held up for half an hour."

"It's okay, Toby." She grabs my shoulders, pulls me towards her, and kisses me on the cheek. "I think I'm getting used to the idea that you're always late."

I'm not sure if the kiss is a friend kiss, or a boyfriend kiss, so I just pat her left shoulder. I can't hug her anyway, as I have the bass in my other hand, and I don't want to put it down. My relief at being reunited with the bass is fading fast. Now I'm just paranoid having it with me. There are a lot of sketchy-looking characters around, and every time one of them glances at me I think they know that I'm holding a bass worth five thousand pounds.

"I was hoping we'd have time to get that second cup of tea." She folds her arms and tips her head from side to side. "We're probably too late, right?"

"I don't know," I say. "Julie told me to be there by four." I shrug to show that I'm not sure of the significance of this fact. "I kind of assumed that it was due to the fact that Live Oak was a dodgy place to be after dark."

Michelle laughs. "Live Oak?" She gives me a comical frown mixed with a smile, then does sidelong looks either way. "This is Live Oak," she says. "Who told you it was dangerous?"

"A bloke called Jasper," I say. "He's the guy who tracked down Julie for me." I switch the bass over to my left hand. It gets heavy quickly. "Maybe we should give the bass back first, and then get tea. To be honest, I want to get rid of it as soon as possible."

"Sounds like a good plan," says Michelle. "Besides, then you won't have to lug it about with you."

I think about telling Michelle how much the bass is worth. Then I decide not to. One stressed-out person in our group is enough. Besides, I can always tell her after I give it back.

Julie's house is only about five minutes from the bus station, and in the opposite direction to Mariner Street. We hurry past used car showrooms, fast food restaurants, and empty shops. Barnard Street itself is lined with crumbling Victorian row houses and empty lots. Number 27 is almost at the top of the hill where it sags between two empty, overgrown lots, like a condemned criminal in front of a firing squad.

The front door is at the top of an ornate set of steps. There's an intercom on the right of the door. Underneath are six buzzers, plus there's one separate bell under the intercom-buzzer set, and another bell on the right side of the door. None of them have any names or numbers.

"Which one is Julie McGuire?" I say. "And which one is the psycho-hatchet-murderer?"

"Hmm." Michelle taps the upper-right buzzer. "This one," she says.

"How can you tell?" I say.

"Just a guess," says Michelle. "It's cleaner than the top left, and she lives on the top floor." She raises her eyebrows. "If the buzzer is cleaner, then someone has been pushing it a lot." She wags her finger at me. "Ex-punk-rocker ladies always get more visitors than psycho-hatchet murderers. Don't they teach you anything in those schools in Port Jackson?"

"The sex life of flowers and French irregular verbs," I say. I shift the bass into my left hand, place my fingertip an inch from the buzzer, and stop. "So I'll follow your judgment on this."

I'm just about to push the buzzer when she grasps my forearm. "Are you sure you really want to do this?" she says. "You don't have to give the bass back."

"Brilliant," I say. Keeping my fingertip an inch from the buzzer, I turn and scrutinize her for a moment. I give her the biggest smile I can muster in order to hide the fact that I'm a little pissed off at her. "You were the one who talked me into this."

"Me?" She spreads the palm of her hand across her collar bones.

"Naturally," I say. "Who else would I be talking about?"

"Please." She holds out her hands and backs away from me slightly. "Don't do this just because of me."

I shake my head. She's right. I don't really want to dump the responsibility onto her. "I want to do it," I say. "Sorry. I'm just a bit agitated."

"Is it because I'm here?" Michelle frowns. "Did you tell her I was coming?"

"No. No way." I take in a long breath. "I'm really glad you're here. I don't think it'll make much difference to Julie."

"I suppose not," she says. "What time is it now?" She rolls her lips over her teeth.

"Late." I raise my arm and push the doorbell. It makes no sound. I stand back and look up at the cracked front of the building, without knowing exactly what I'm looking for. Maybe someone leaning out.

"Aargh!" Michelle does a pretend scream, squeezes my upper arm with both hands, and pushes her head against my shoulder. "How could I be stupid? Hatchet murderers get more callers, of course!"

I don't know why or how I do this; I twist toward her while she's still holding onto my arm. Then I lean down and brush my lips against hers.

She increases the pressure on my arm. "Hiya," she says. "Do I know you by any chance?"

"I think we met," I say. I lean down, and give her a lingering kiss.

"Hello!" The harsh intercom voice jerks me back to reality like an alarm clock. "Is that Toby?"

I pull back from Michelle, but breaking away is too sudden, so I lean my forehead against hers while I speak. "Yes. It's Toby," I say. It's an odd sensation speaking to a disembodied voice on an intercom while I'm gazing into

Michelle's eyes. "My friend Michelle is here as well. Is that okay?"

"Fine," says the voice on the intercom. "Come right up."

The door buzzes. I lean on it, and it opens inward. I switch hands with the bass yet again, and usher Michelle in ahead of me. As she passes, I kiss her one more time.

31
TUESDAY

"I wish you'd come a bit earlier." A voice echoes down the stairwell to the lobby. I look up to see where the voice is coming from, and get a kind of reverse vertigo. The staircase winds upward, past giant doorways, crumbling pillars, and cherubs with their wings and noses knocked off.

"I don't think this place was built with ex-punk-rockers and axe murderers in mind," whispers Michelle as we climb.

"Why are you whispering?" I say.

"Maybe there are some archdukes taking a nap," she says, pointing to one of the doorways as we pass.

"Sorry to rush you," says Julie, as we reach the top floor.

Until this morning, I didn't even know if Julie McGuire was alive or dead. Now here she is right in front of me, all in black, in sharp contrast to faded greens and browns of the walls and doorways.

"I was hoping we'd have a bit more time." She pushes open her door, which is about twice as tall as she is. "I have to go somewhere and I'm late already."

Maybe this explains why she's so dressed up.

"Sorry we're late," I say as I stand aside to let Michelle go in first. "The bus got stuck in a traffic jam."

The hallway is pretty narrow, one side being taken up by an overflowing bookcase.

"Oh, well, can't be helped," says Julie. She leans forward and gives Michelle a peck on the cheek as she passes. "Aren't you pretty?" she says.

Michelle's cheeks go red. "Thanks," she says, as she squeezes past a fragile-looking table with a phone on it.

"Just a statement of fact," says Julie. "I'm just staying here at the moment while I'm moving out of my flat. I don't normally live in this level of squalor."

In spite of the shambles, the place is actually pretty clean except for a slight background pong. The smell is familiar, but I can't quite place it until something soft nudges my leg.

"Oh, don't let the cats out," Julie says.

I look down and wedge a morbidly obese ginger cat against the wall with my leg. Julie stoops down and wedges the football-cat under her elbow. "Come in, Madison," she says. "Otherwise you'll be spending the night in the hall."

With the cat under one arm, she wraps the other arm around my neck and kisses me on the cheek. "It's so nice to meet you, finally." She dances across the floor like a soccer player as she tries to maneuver a calico cat away from the door. "Come into my studio." I squeeze in past owner and cats into a slightly more intense cat-pong.

I make my way down the hall to a kitchen jammed with books. Books on chairs, books on tables, books on the floor.

"Let me see, let me see!" says Julie.

She bustles past me, lifts a pile of books off the table, and distributes the books onto other stacks on the floor and the couch.

"Sorry about the clutter." She splays her fingers on the table as if it's a piano. "Why don't you plonk it down here?"

"Oh, wow," says Michelle, picking a paperback off one of the piles. "My mum reads Ruth Rendell books."

"Honey." Julie spins around. "Please don't mess things up," she says. "There's actually an order to these."

I lower the case gently onto the table. After the Rupert incident at the beach it seems to have developed some uneven edges, and I don't want it to scratch the tabletop.

"Whoa." Julie turns back to me, and presses her palms together as if she's praying. "You know I hadn't really thought much about this." She blows out a long breath and rests her chin on her raised fingertips. Her hands are heavily veined. They look a lot older than her face. "I'm kinda nervous."

"Yeah." I shake my arms to get the blood flowing again after the weight of the bass. "Me too."

"You know what?" she says. "It really is a weird situation." She flips up the catches—one, two, three—and raises the lid as if the case contains holy relics, and maybe it does in a way.

She whistles.

Michelle comes around from behind me. "I forgot how beautiful it was," she says.

"Yup," says Julie, and lets out a short laugh. "Pretty, and a pain in the arse."

She gives Michelle a harsh glance, and just for a moment, I'm not completely certain that she's referring to the bass.

Julie looks down at the bass and takes in a long breath. "I never thought I'd see this again." She puts her hands back into her prayer position. "You don't know anything about this instrument, do you?"

"Just that my brother came home with it one night," I say. "He gave it to me when he went away," I add quickly. "It wasn't him who stole it. He paid for it. He bought it about eighteen months ago." I have to clear my throat. I'm not a good liar. Of course, I don't know for certain that he didn't steal it, but now I'm guessing that he might well have done just that.

"Oh. I know who stole it." Julie lifts the instrument out of its case. Without looking at me she says, "I know exactly who stole it." She rests the body on the table and slides a veined hand up the neck as if she's stroking one of her cats. She smiles at me. "It wasn't you, and it wasn't your brother." She plays a few notes.

The intonation is clumsy, and the timing is off, but it's just about recognizable as "Day Tripper." She's no Paul McCartney, but she's better than either Rupert or Shawn.

"Nice," I say. I'm getting better at lying.

She purses her lips as she looks at me. "Now you." She passes the bass over to me.

"Last time," I say. I put my foot up on a chair, prop the body on my leg, and play the same lines. It really is the last time, so I throw in every slide, trill, and decoration I can think of. Probably the best I've ever played it.

Julie bends down and scoops up the calico cat. "That"—she gestures toward my fingers with the puzzled-looking cat—"is nice."

"It's okay," I say.

"You know what's funny?" She strokes the top of the cat's head with her chin. "Over the years I must have heard a hundred people play that instrument." The cat begins to purr loudly. "Every single one played a Beatles riff when they picked it up." The cat flails its legs, and Julie places it back on the floor. "Uncanny. Right?"

"I suppose," I say. I offer the instrument back to Julie, but when she places her hands on it I have to make a real effort to let go of it. I want to leave before I change my mind. "I don't want to be rude, but we need to get going.

If you don't have the reward money, then it doesn't matter." I have a sudden urge to grab the bass back, so I step away and thrust my fingers into my pockets. "But if you did have it, the money would come in handy."

"How would you feel if instead of giving you a reward"—Julie runs her fingers down the strings—"I just gave the bass right back to you?"

This completely throws me, but before I can speak Julie says, "This probably sounds mad, but the bass has been bad luck for me."

With impressive speed the calico cat jumps on to the table and settles into the case. Julie ushers it aside with the back of her free hand. "It's been stolen more than once," she says. She places the instrument in its case, but the cat immediately settles down on top of it, as if it's the most comfortable bed in the world.

"The first person who stole it was a girl." She points at Michelle. "Younger than you, sweetheart." She turns back to me. "She was a Beatles fan—a groupie really—and she stole it from George Harrison."

I gasp. "This was George Harrison's bass!"

Julie picks up the cat. "Let me tell the story," she says. "George invited her to Abbey Road Studios." The cat blinks as Julie scratches its head. "They were going to go out for the evening, but the group was working on 'Back in the USSR.' A sales rep showed up at about ten p.m. with some free samples of Fender guitars and basses, one of which was this." She taps the case. "Paul was intending to play bass, but he was busy working on the piano part, so he asked George to play some bass lines, and he used this instrument.

"When he was done, he left it on a couch next to the groupie. She fell asleep while she was waiting. She woke up some time later. It was three a.m., and the band was still playing and shouting at one another. The girl was pissed off that George had left her waiting, and it was pretty obvious that he wasn't going to take her out, so she quietly picked up the bass and walked home with it.

"When she woke up the next afternoon she was racked with guilt, but what could she do? She could hardly take it back at that point. Eventually she taught herself to play it." Julie grins. "Not terribly well, as you just heard."

"You were the groupie?" says Michelle.

"Bingo," says Julie without looking at her.

"But why do you think it's unlucky?" I say.

"That was the high watermark of my life." She taps the case again. "Aged fourteen." She clasps her hands in front of her chest. "In spite of being a fairly lame musician I got into a number of bands, partly based on the fact that I had George Harrison's bass, and partly because I was cute." Now she does look at Michelle. She shakes her head. "Boy, you should have seen me back then, sweetheart."

Julie turns back to me. "That was the sum total of my life." She nods her head. "Then along comes your brother. One way or another he gets the bass, and voilà. My luck changes overnight. The very next day—and I swear to God

I'm not making this up—I get a publishing deal for a book I'd been working on for about five years."

"That is amazing," says Michelle.

"The day after that"—she stabs her finger at Michelle—"I file for a divorce from my deadbeat husband." She plays a drumbeat on the edge of the bass.

"Divorce isn't lucky," I say.

"Trust me, honey," says Julie. "Divorce isn't always a bad thing. So." She bends down while still holding the cat, plucks a toy mouse off the floor, and dangles it by its tail in front of the cat. "Call me a superstitious fool, but I'm not quite as enthusiastic about getting the bass back as you might think."

"Couldn't you sell it?" I say.

She shakes her head. "I'm done with it," she says. "It's not one of the really valuable ones."

"But it was George Harrison's," says Michelle. "That must make it worth thousands."

"Aren't you the clever one," says Julie, "but you only have my word for it. To sell it based on the fact that George Harrison once touched it, you would need to authenticate it at one of the big auction houses like Sotheby's." She lifts the cat above her head as if it's some kind of sacrifice. The cat doesn't seem to mind. "No receipts. No authentication. Nothing distinctive about the bass, really. Poor old George is no longer with us to verify anything. Worst-case scenario, Sotheby's checks the serial number and finds out that it was stolen. They give it back to Fender-CBS, and

Fender-CBS put in a glass case in some executive's office where nobody ever looks at it."

"I thought possession was nine-tenths of the law," I say.

"Between you and me perhaps." Julie makes a coughing laugh. "Between one of us and a multi-national corporation, probably not."

"If you really don't want it, then I'll keep it," I say.

"Deal." Holding the cat in one hand, she latches the case with the other, lifts it off the table, and holds it out with the handle pointed toward me. "Thank you for letting me see it again." She drops the cat to the floor, takes my hand, then closes my fingers around the case handle.

Just as she does this there's a loud buzz, which makes me jump. Then I realize it's the doorbell. I turn to look down the hall and catch Michelle's eyes. She smiles at me.

I turn my attention back to Julie. She seems to have aged ten years in just a few seconds.

She's standing. "Crap." She is no longer smiling. "Toby, I wish you'd gotten here earlier," she says. "Take the bass and go. Right now. Don't argue." She pushes Michelle and me toward the door. "It was a stolen bass, but now I'm giving it back to you. It is no longer a stolen bass."

I'm not sure whether I really should keep the bass, but she steps out of my reach, giving me no choice in the matter.

"Let's hope that giving it away creates good karma." Julie makes her way back into the hall. "Hi," she says into the intercom. Her voice sounds different than when she buzzed me in. She sounds her age. She turns to me. "Toby, please leave right now." She opens the door and stands by it. "Bye, bye. Michelle, it was nice to meet you."

32
TUESDAY

We squeeze past Julie into the hall.

I look down at the bass, then I grin at Michelle and laugh. I can't believe that everything worked out so well. I turn to the doorway to say thank you, but I'm distracted by footsteps thundering up the stairs behind me. I turn around to see the last person I wanted to see.

"Hey, my brother!" he says. "It is a pleasure to see you." He looks from me to Michelle, and down at the case. "What unexpected delights rain down on us."

"Hi Rupert," I say. Each time I see him he's wearing one less item of clothing. This time he's not wearing a shirt. He's so lean that he looks like an anatomical diagram with every muscle sharply defined. I hope this is the last time I see him.

"Toby and Michelle were just leaving, Rupert," says Julie.

"And you came bearing gifts." Rupert's arm ripples as he points at the case. "Would I be right in assuming that you have in your hand a precision bass?"

"Yup," I say, a little sheepishly. "It's the same one."

"You have returned that which was lost to its rightful home." His face crumples into a smile, which somehow looks wrong with the sunglasses and the pork pie hat. "You are a man of honor. All the muses in heaven thank you."

"Actually I'm taking it away," I say.

His smile fades a little. "Taking it away. Bringing it back." He shrugs. "It's all the same in the end. It's the music that remains." He jabs a finger at me. "Hey, do you think I could see it one last time? Just for posterity?"

"I suppose." I look from Rupert, to Michelle, to Julie.

I'm just about to kneel down, open the case, and let Rupert have one last look when Julie says, "They have to catch a bus, Rupert."

"Women! Can you believe it?" Rupert glares at me and knits his eyebrows. "Always in a panic about something." He looks at me as if he expects me to agree with him. "There's always another bus. Am I right, Toby? Or am I right?" His eyes light up. "Hey, why don't you come back inside. I have some Emerson Lake & Palmer CDs. Awesome bass playing. Greg Lake. You've never heard of him; you're way too young. I consider it my solemn duty to educate you in the knowledge of great bass players."

"Actually I do need to get to the bus station," I say. I make a silent prayer that Rupert's car has broken down or something. I do not want him to offer me a lift.

"Time and tide wait for no man," says Rupert. "May the wings of the angels bring you a safe journey and a safe return." He shuffles over to the banisters, leaving room for us to get past. "All I ask is that you leave a little of the joy you brought with you."

I stand to one side to let Michelle go first. She jogs down the steps, past Rupert, then stops to wait for me. I begin to follow. Just as I pass Rupert, I reach out to shake his hand. I can't say I'll ever think of him as a friend, but at least things have ended up okay with him.

Rupert doesn't take my hand, though. Instead he slides back across the stairs, blocking my exit and cutting me off from Michelle.

A dark shape scuttles past my feet and dives down the stairs. It stops, crouches down on a step between Rupert and Michelle, and begins to lick one of its paws.

"Lex!" cries Julie. "Rupert, can you grab Lexington?"

Rupert looks Michelle up and down, then studies the cat for a moment but makes no move to pick it up.

"Please, Rupert," says Julie. "He'll be stuck out there yowling all night."

"Okay, let's quit the pantomime," says Rupert. With

what is now a familiar move, he swings his arm behind him, reaches into his back pocket, and pulls out his Stanley knife.

"I think you should give the bass to me." He holds the knife down and away from his leg, then slides out the shiny blade.

Michelle picks up the cat and holds it out toward Julie, but with Rupert blocking her, she can't reach.

I offer yet another silent prayer that she doesn't try to take the knife away from Rupert. Any more prayers and I'm going to end up being religious.

"Rupert," says Julie, "just let him leave."

"It's Toby's bass," says Michelle.

Rupert swivels around to look at her, keeping the knife by his leg.

"It's not yours," Michelle continues. The cat wriggles, jumps out of her grip, and flops onto the stairs. "Toby came to give it back, but Julie told him he could keep it."

"Is it Toby's bass?" says Rupert. "Or is it Julie's bass? You don't seem too sure of yourself, my friend."

"Rupert, shut the hell up!" says Julie.

"Oh, so it's shut-up-Rupert time." Rupert tosses the knife in the air with the blade still out. It spins a couple of times and he catches it by the handle. "I was just having a pleasant conversation with this young woman here, and all of a sudden it's shut-up-Rupert time."

"It is Toby's bass," says Julie.

I listen to a motorcycle passing out on the street below.

Rupert takes a step toward me, presses his free hand

against my chest, and points to the bass with the knife. "I'm afraid that this item is not leaving with you. It belongs to my wife."

"Ex-wife," says Julie. "He's just a kid, Rupert. Let him go."

"Soon-to-be ex-wife." Rupert brings his face close to mine. He still has the cheesy smell of cigarettes. He brings the knife up next to my cheek. The shiny blade reflects a beam of light that flickers across his face.

I want to be afraid, but I'm not. This just doesn't seem real.

"I gave him the bass." Julie's voice seems to come from a long way off. "It belongs to him now. Just let him go."

"Nope," says Rupert. "Love, honor, and obey. Giving something away. Giving something valuable away. Giving something valuable to a complete stranger should be a joint decision for a married couple."

He brings the blade closer to my face. I can feel the sharp metal against the side of my nose.

"Fair is fair, Toby." Rupert's mouth opens and closes, showing his yellow teeth. "You're a man; you're probably going to get married at some point. Do you want your wife to make important financial decisions without consulting you first?"

"No. I don't," I say.

"Rupert, just let him go," says Julie.

Rupert looks up at her, as if he's actually considering doing what Julie says. Then steps off to one side.

"Run back to Port Jackson, Toby," he says.

I take one step, then another. The third step brings me level with him. With the fourth step, I'm past him. I'm just about to break into a run when a steel claw fastens onto my wrist. I wince, expecting to feel the knife slash at my face, but instead my hand is twisted backward. I have no choice but to let go of the case, and it falls onto the stairs.

The next moment I'm gripped around my upper arm and shoved down the stairs. For a second I think I'm going to go headlong down three floors, but Michelle catches me.

"A Fender Precision Bass." I turn to see Rupert triumphant at the top of the stairs. He picks up the heavy case as if it weighs nothing. "How much do you think it's worth?" With his other hand he slides the blade back into the knife and returns it to his back pocket.

I know that Rupert is going to sell the bass, but I'll be hanged if he's going to get several thousand for it. "It's not a very good one," I say. "It's worth maybe two or three hundred pounds."

"A Fender? Two or three hundred?" says Rupert. "How about five or six hundred? Let's call it seven hundred for you thinking I'm dumb enough to believe it was only worth two hundred."

"Rupert," says Julie. "You're going straight down to the pub, and somebody's going to give you a hundred quid for it."

Rupert grins at Julie. "That's the fun part," he says. "Some punter will give me a hundred, but he'll sell it for a grand." Rupert looks back at me. "I'm just cutting out the middle man, Toby. You can have the bass back if you give me seven hundred pounds, or you can give some punter a thousand. Can you see what I'm doing? I'm giving you a bass and putting three hundred quid in your pocket. You will never get another opportunity like this."

"Where's he going to get seven hundred pounds?" says Julie.

"He's a Londoner," says Rupert. "He's got a bundle stashed away some place." Rupert looks at me. "That's right, isn't it?"

"I don't have seven hundred pounds," I say. "I don't even have seven." I turn and walk down the stairs. Julie is right. The bass is cursed. Maybe you have to give it away to get rid of the curse. Maybe this is for the best.

33
TUESDAY

"I don't understand why you don't go to the police," says Michelle from her seat on the opposite edge of the lifeguard platform to me.

In the darkness, I can just make out the white top of a wave before it thuds into the sand a few yards in front of us.

"What would we tell them?" I turn and study her silhouette as the breeze makes her hair flutter. "Doesn't there have to be a crime to report?"

The night is fractured by a silent sheet of lightning that snakes across the horizon, igniting the edges of humungous clouds and turning the distant sky into something that looks like a vision of heaven in an old painting.

Michelle is only sitting a few inches away from me, but the gap is empty space, and she might as well be as far away as wherever the thunderstorm is taking place. She's probably completely ashamed of me for letting Rupert walk off with my most-treasured possession.

"It's your bass." Her silhouette shifts as she turns toward me. "Rupert threatened you, and then he stole it."

Something buzzes past my face. I swat it away.

"Threatening and stealing are against the law," she says.

"I don't know," I say. "Maybe the police might say that the bass was his." A wall of surf thumps on the sand a few yards away. "You know, possession is nine-tenths of the law. Anyway, I think it's difficult to get the police to respond to a threat, especially when the threat is over."

"But you can prove that the bass is yours." Michelle's silhouette is lit up by another sheet of lightning. "Just show them the receipt."

Two human figures walk along the shoreline in front of us. I can barely see them in the gloom. "It's not quite that simple," I say.

"Do you think they're going for a night-time dip?" Michelle points to the shadowy figures.

"No," I say. "I think they're just out for a stroll."

"If it's your brother's bass," she says. "He must have a receipt somewhere, from when he bought it."

"I'm pretty certain that he bought it from Rupert." I

study the string of small lights that stretch across the bay. I suppose they're fishing boats. I wonder if they're afraid of the storm. Or maybe it's heading away from us. Can I actually bring myself to say this? If I reveal that there's a thief in my family then she'll never be interested in me again. Not that it matters now. Nothing is going to happen this evening, and this was my last chance. "Either that or he stole it from Rupert."

There I've said it. I turn and study Michelle's profile as the surf booms onto the sand, expecting her to make some excuse, jump down from the platform, and go home. But she doesn't. Maybe I should qualify my last statement.

"Knowing Rupert, I doubt he'd let anyone steal from him." I take a long breath. "Shawn paid for it, but he bought it knowing full well that it was stolen. I remember the night he came home with it. The description of the bloke more or less matches Rupert."

Michelle gives a hollow laugh. "Yeah. Let's go back and ask Rupert for a receipt."

A stream of lights appear off to our left, sprinkling blue and yellow reflections over the water.

"That's the London train on the Bay Bridge," she says.

"Pretty," I say. "I was thinking of going back and seeing Rupert, actually."

"You'll probably be on that tomorrow," she says. "That is, if you're still alive." She shifts around in the seat so she's facing me. "I'll kill you if you go back to Rupert's."

"Really. Why?" I say. "Don't you think I should have tried harder to wrestle the bass back from him?"

Michelle stares at me for a moment. "No. Not at all," she says. "He's a psycho. Please don't go back. He's the kind of bloke you read about in the papers."

Something tickles the underside of my arm. I flinch, thinking it's an insect, then I relax when I realize it's a set of fingertips. Then I tense up when I realize who's fingertips are on my arm. A moment ago I was half asleep. Now my heart is pounding. Her fingertips slide across the inside of my wrist and interlace between my own fingers. There's a rustle of fabric on wood as Michelle slides across the six inches toward me. The lightning flickers again, then it's blotted out by Michelle's silhouette. I breathe in her chai tea scent, then warm, soft lips are pressed against my mouth, and fingers find their way under my arms and around my ribcage.

After some time Michelle pulls away, slides under my arm, and pulls me close to her, making one side of me very warm, and the other side chilly in the night air.

"Will you come and see me off tomorrow?" I reach behind her head and smooth her hair against the back of her scalp.

She shifts her head around, kisses me again, and says, "You know, I've lived here all my life, and I've never been night swimming."

"That's probably true of most Brunswickers," I say. "I mean here we are on a warm night and nobody's swimming."

"Have you ever done it?" she says. "Don't tell me. Every night the sea at Port Jackson is full of Port Jacksonites splashing around."

"I have been swimming at night," I say. "And it was in Port Jackson, and I was on my own." I don't tell her when I swam at night, or anything about why I did it, or that it wasn't really a choice.

"Weren't you afraid of sharks?" she says.

"I didn't really think about it," I say. "Not at first anyway. To be honest I don't think there are any sharks around here. There are rip tides though."

"No." She snuggles closer to me. "No sharks at night. They're all tucked up in the sea bed." Suddenly she pulls away from me and sits up. "Come on. Let's go for a swim. It's warm. It's calm. It's a perfect night."

A hollow feeling floods through me. "There's a storm coming." I manage to lift my arm and point past her to the horizon just as the lightning flickers again.

"No thunder though," she says. "Probably one hundred miles away."

"And we don't have swimsuits," I say.

"My underwear is pretty presentable," she says, and without waiting for any more of my excuses, she jumps down onto the sand. She staggers for a moment to get her balance, then says, "You are wearing underwear, aren't you?" She leans on the side of the platform and levers a sneaker off one foot with the toe of the other foot. "You're not the commando type, are you?"

I am now completely empty. The only thing inside me is my heart hammering. I slide off the seat and drop down onto the sand just as Michelle crosses her arms in front of her and pulls her T-shirt over her head. I try not to stare at her light-colored bra as I unfasten my jeans. I turn away, but out of the corner of my eye I can't help seeing the darker circles in the middle of each bra cup.

I also try not to look as she bends forward to slide off her jeans. I have just enough time to pull off my shirt before she is beside me. I can feel warmth radiating off her as she interlocks her fingers with mine. With legs that are almost completely numb, I lead her across the twenty or so yards of beach to the wet sand.

"Are you a strong swimmer?" she says.

I risk one glance at Michelle, and at that very moment the storm flickers, and for half a second one side of her glows blue. I have no idea what she meant when she told me her underwear was presentable. She certainly didn't mean modest or chaste.

"I'm okay," I say. I wait for one wave to break, then gently guide her forward onto the cool, soft sand. The next wave is waist high. It knocks us both off balance. I flounder back and forth, pulling Michelle with me. I really think we're going to make it, but then the third wave hits and sweeps us onto our backs. I spring to my feet. Michelle lets go of my hand, puts her arm around my back, and we run back up the beach.

Once we're on dry sand, I slide my arm around her

back. She holds onto my shoulder blades and pulls me toward her.

"Isn't there any way you can stay here?" she says. "I'm going to miss you."

"I don't know," I say. "Not really. I'm going to miss you too." I slide my fingers up her spine, but there's no strap. Not only is her bra not presentable, it isn't even a bra.

It's a bikini mark.

34
TUESDAY

I have a plan.

The first part of the plan is that I tell Michelle I'm getting on the ten o'clock bus to Port Jackson.

That goes off without a hitch.

The second part of the plan is that I say goodbye to Michelle, then get on the bus. Once I'm on the bus I watch her leave the bus station, then as soon as she's out of sight, I get back off the bus and make my way back to Julie's building.

That seems to go okay as well.

The third part of the plan is that I go up to Julie's flat,

persuade Rupert to give me back the bass, then return to the bus station in time to catch the last bus, which leaves at eleven.

Like all good plans, it's simple, but maybe it's a little too simple. Maybe I should have worked out a few of the details and prepared myself for some variables.

The first variable is that Julie's neighborhood at night has very little in common with her neighborhood during the day. A group of three heavyset gents in black hoodies throw pretend karate kicks at each other on the corner of her street.

Several sirens swell and fade. The karate gents are using the entire width of the sidewalk as their dojo. I'm just about to cross to the opposite side of the street when a police car and an ambulance fly past with their lights flickering.

I change my mind about crossing over. In the blue glow, I catch sight of a biker with his arm around the waist of a girl not much older than Michelle. A few yards farther, a kid on a mini-motorcycle is tossing brick-sized bags in through the open window of an SUV.

I have no choice but to brave the karate gents. There's a yell. One of them stumbles backward across the sidewalk and slams into a street lamp. He looks like he's in a film being played backward, and speeded up. Under the right circumstances I'd probably find this funny.

These are not the right circumstances. I don't even want to smile in this part of town, let alone laugh.

The guy folds forward to catch his breath.

This is probably my best chance. I march toward them. Just as I'm about level, the one who was catching his breath snaps upright and charges back at the other two. He's just about to plow right over me when he stops.

"Alright, mate," he says, and nods at me.

His expression is not so much fear, as uncertainty. He has no idea who I am. He's as scared of me as I am of him.

Makes no sense.

Finally, I arrive at Julie's driveway. I stop at the gate, and scan the front garden. It's pitch black, apart from the few streaks of light that have managed to filter through the bushes. I move into the shadows by the gate, and give my eyes time to adjust. A jumble of different styles of music and TV shows spill down into the front garden and merge with the distant roar of traffic and sirens. It reminds me a little of the Beatles's "Revolution Number Nine," from *The White Album*.

A flurry of pops erupts in the distance. I don't like to think about what they are.

When I'm satisfied that nobody's lying in wait for me, I make my way up to the front door. This is it. This is as far my plan goes. Rush up the stairs, kick Julie's door in, and take Rupert by surprise. Somehow it slipped my mind that I'd have to kick the street door in as well. Now that I'm here, I don't really want to kick anybody's door in. I would have repaired Julie's door for her, but I don't want to be responsible for repairing the street door as well. All-night carpentry isn't one of my strong points. Especially in a war zone.

On the other hand, this door looks so flimsy that it seems like even an outburst of strong language would probably knock it off its hinges. First I lean on it, but it stays put. I try pushing, but pushing gets me no farther than leaning. Finally, I shove my shoulder into it as if I'm going into a rugby scrum, but all I get is a sore shoulder.

My last resort. My finger hovers over Julie's bell. So much for surprise. Not that my idea was that much of a good idea in the first place.

I push the bell.

I wait for the voice on the intercom. Will it be Julie? Or will it be Rupert? And which of them will be less pleased that I've come visiting?

But there's no voice on the intercom. Just a scream from one of the TVs. It's a man screaming. For some reason, I find this more disturbing than the sound of a woman screaming. What's even more disturbing is that I'm not 100 percent certain that the scream came from a TV.

I need to rethink this. Maybe I should just go home. I'm just on the point of turning around, heading for the bus station, when I hear voices. A moment later a couple staggers through the gateway. They're the Hells Angel and the much younger girl I saw out in the street.

The girl stops and studies the front of the building. Seeing her up close, she's not actually as young as I thought when I saw her earlier.

"Got your key?" she says to the angel.

"Shit," he says as he pats his pockets down.

"Just as well, I remembered mine," says the girl, waving her key ring. "You'd forget your head if it wasn't fastened on."

I move off to one side as she runs past me up the steps. She glances at me. I smile at her, but she doesn't smile back. I move even farther to the side as the guy sways past me. He smells even worse than the toilet-changing-room at the Jubliee Cinema. He burps, but doesn't look at me.

The woman unlocks the door and sashays inside. The man follows her. He lets the door swing shut behind him. I strain my ears, but I don't hear the click of the latch. I give them a moment to get upstairs, then I try the door again. This time it swings open and I step into the greenish light of the lobby.

35
TUESDAY

I stay back in the shadows while the Hell's Angel hauls himself to the top of the first flight of stairs. He stops and stretches when he reaches the landing, and then disappears through an open door. Just as he shuts the door there's a pop, and everything goes black.

Fantastic. One more thing I didn't factor into my plans. The hall lights are on time switches.

It really is pitch black, so I push the front door open a fraction. This throws an eerie glow across everything, which is not quite bright enough to make out any details. I slide my hand along the wall until I find the time switch.

It's one of the push-button kind. I punch it, and the darkness is replaced once again by a greenish gloom.

I wonder how long the light is going to stay on. If the Hell's Angel punched the switch as soon as he got through the door, and then the light went off just as he got inside his flat, then the lights must stay on for about a minute.

Sounds about right.

Just to make sure I get my full minute, I wait for the light to go off, and then hit the switch again. The light flickers on with a loud clicking sound, and I head up the first flight of stairs as softly as I can. I go especially softly past the Hell's Angel's door.

I wait for the downstairs light to pop off, then I hit the second floor switch and run up to the next flight. I go through the same procedure at the third set, and then I'm on the little top-floor landing, which has only one door. Julie's.

I lean over the banisters. This must have been quite a fancy building at one time. The stairs spiral down and round, like the inside of a shell, before coming to an end on the black-and-white tiled floor about forty feet below. I was wrong about the lights staying on for a minute. The second floor light is still on. They must stay on for random amounts of time.

It seems quiet up here, and I get the feeling there's nobody home. I press my ear against the door. The wooden surface is cool and smooth. I can't hear anything, although it's difficult to be sure with the clicking sound of the light. I stand back. There are three slow clicks, and then the light pops off. It's not totally dark though. The light from the second floor is still on, and I can just make out that there's another light switch next to the door.

I punch the switch, and shove the door.

It feels really solid. I guess kicking doors off their hinges isn't really my thing. Perhaps if I'd invited a couple of the karate guys from down on the street and brought them up here with me. Maybe then I might have a chance of forcing the door open.

But me on my own? Not a chance. I reckon I could easily break my ankle if I tried kicking it open.

The clicking noise slows down, and a moment later the light pops off. I punch the switch again, and almost at exactly the same moment the street door bangs shut downstairs.

I lean over the banisters and look straight down the spiral stairwell. I hear footsteps cross the tiles, but whoever it is remains hidden by the stairs. The sound of a man clearing his throat echoes upward, and that sound is followed by footsteps pounding up the first set of stairs. The second-floor light comes on and more footsteps, closer this time.

The third-floor light snaps on, and finally I get a brief look at him. I spring away from the banister and flatten myself against the wall. It's a man with no shirt, carrying something long and shiny. The landing I'm on has only one feature. Julie's doorway. Nowhere to hide. I catch a glance of Rupert's pork pie hat as he mounts the third flight of stairs. I crouch down so I'm out of his line of sight.

The footsteps slow.

Has he seen me?

Has he slowed down because he's out of breath?

Or does he just know I'm here out of instinct?

Three more footsteps. He's almost at the top. I catch a glimpse of the pork pie hat, then, click … click … click. The overhead light snaps off.

"Shit," says Rupert.

As for me, if I wasn't trying to hide I could say the same thing. It's not completely dark. There's a glow from downstairs. Probably the second-floor light. I look up. Rupert is outlined in a perfect silhouette in front of me. I can even make out his sunglasses. Grasped in one hand is the p-bass.

He has to be able to see me, and yet he doesn't say anything to me?

"Shit," he says again, but not to me as far I can tell. He reaches into his pocket and pulls something out. A knife? My heart pounds, but it's only a key.

He can't see me. It's totally insane. It could barely be described as dark up here.

Then I get it.

The sunglasses! I'm not sure which of us is the bigger fool. Him or me. He balances the bass across the top of the banisters, then reaches forward and prods around the door frame. I guess he's looking for the switch. Just at that moment the downstairs light goes off.

Now we really are in the dark. If I have any chance at all, then this is it. I spring to my feet. "Hi, Rupert," I say.

"Good sir," he says.

I angle myself toward the sound of his voice, bend forward, and ram the top of my head into something that feels too hard to be Rupert's stomach.

"Jesus!" he yells. For a second nothing happens. I'm about to ram him again when something that sounds like a heavy suitcase goes tumbling down the stairs.

There's another sound—wood sliding on wood—and then the sound of one of the stair rods snapping.

I have just enough time for one breath when I hear the worst sound of all. It's the sound of something heavy hitting the tiles in the lobby. It's a sharp, splintering crack, a little like the sound a whip makes but with a kind of musical throb underneath it.

I punch the light. A shirtless figure lies crumpled a dozen stairs below me. "Rupert," I say. For a second I think I've killed him, but then he looks up at me.

"Good evening, good sir," he says.

It's Rupert's voice, but I hardly recognize him without the sunglasses. He has the saddest eyes I've ever seen.

"Are you all right?" I say. I come down a couple of steps, but I don't want to get too close, as he may still be dangerous.

He points toward one of his feet. "I don't think I'll make the football season this year."

I follow his finger and notice that he seems to have a

shoe on backward. The snapping sound I heard wasn't a banister. It was Rupert's ankle. He must be in agony, but he's just lying there as if he decided to take a nap halfway up the stairs.

"Where's Julie?" I say.

"She's at work," he says, and then I notice the slur in his words. I don't know what Rupert's been dosing himself with, but it's got to be one hell of a painkiller.

Something shiny catches my eye. The key is lying on the landing. Rupert must have dropped it when I hit him. I pick it up. "I'll go in and call an ambulance," I say, holding up the key.

"Very decent of you," he says.

I unlock Julie's door, find the phone, and call for the emergency services. I give them the address, tell them the front door is open, then go back to the landing.

"Help is on its way," I tell him, then look over the banisters again.

Far below, shattered on the tiled floor, with its neck splintered, its body smashed, and the whole thing held together only by its strings, is the p-bass.

I stare at it.

Even like this it's beautiful.

Like a sculpture.

"I wasn't going to hurt you." Rupert's voice cuts into my thoughts. "I just wanted the bass back."

"That's nice to know," I say. I tear myself away from

the sight of the p-bass and sit down on the top step. I still don't believe him.

"I just wanted the bass back," he says. He shifts and draws in a sharp breath. "That's all I wanted to do. I just wanted to play bass in a band."

"You have an unusual way of going about it," I say. "Why couldn't you just buy a cheap bass and learn to play it like everyone else does?"

"Once you've played a bass that was owned by George Harrison, you can't go back to any old bass," he says. "Can you imagine how sad that would be?"

I can imagine it, but I try not to. "You believe that?" I say. "Was it really George Harrison's?"

"I think it was," he says. "Who the hell knows for sure?" He tries to shift his position again. "In the end, who cares?"

I'm not sure what to say to this, but I don't have to say anything as a siren sounds outside on the street.

The siren becomes almost deafening, and then stops. There's a flurry of voices and radios, then someone hammers on the downstairs door.

I hit the light again, then I make my way down the stairs. I vault over Rupert without touching him, and jog the rest of the way down. As I pass his door, the Hell's Angel pokes his head out.

Down in the lobby, I step over what's left of the bass and open the door. Three ambulance men barge in, almost pushing me over. I point up the stairs. "He's on the third floor," I say. The ambulance men thunder up the stairs with their radios chattering. More people have come out to look. Heads peer over the banisters.

I look down at what's left of the bass.

Not even Harry Haller could fix this.

I stack the pieces together, being careful not to get any splinters. The head has come away from the neck, but the strings are still attached. I wind them around everything to keep it all together, then stuff the whole thing under my arm.

A moment later I'm outside. I don't have much time to get to the bus stop, but I have one last call to make. I jog back past where I saw the karate guys, past where I saw the kid on the mini-bike, and finally get back to the boardwalk.

The tide has come in and the waves are lapping at the foot of the lifeguard stand. Ignoring my wet feet, I wade across to the stand and clamber up onto the platform. I watch the sky flicker for a moment. I wait for a fair-sized wave to roll in, then I swing my arm back and hurl the bass out as far as it'll go.

I take a long breath, and then I hear the splash. Sounds like it was one of my better throws.

I jump back down to the beach and head for the bus station. I wonder what'll happen to the bass. I don't even know if it'll sink or float. If it floats, maybe it'll wash out to sea and end up in France. Maybe it could even float back to America where it came from.

Five minutes later I'm on the bus, heading back to Port Jackson.

36
WEDNESDAY

The next morning I'm woken by a soft tap on the door. Mom pokes her head around the corner.

"I thought I'd find you in here," she says as she comes in, carrying two cups of tea.

For a second I'm a little confused. Shawn's room looks entirely different without all the musical equipment strewn across it.

Then I get my bearings.

"I think this is yours." She plonks one of the teacups on my bedside table, then sits down on the end of the bed. "I have some good news and some bad news." She slurps her tea, then pulls a face. "Yuck. I think this is yours." She leans over to the bedside table and switches the cups, then returns to her seat at the end of the bed. "Which would you like first, the good or the bad?"

"The bad, I suppose." I scoot myself up into a semi-upright position. "It's probably not worth breaking the steady flow of badness, midstream." I turn the cup around so that I don't drink from the same side, then take a sip. It's pretty decent.

Mom yawns and covers her mouth. "You're going to have to go to school today, young fellow-me-lad."

A number of questions filter through my sleep-addled brain, but I let them flit away. "Okay," I say. "I can just about live with that. What's the good news?"

Mom scratches her cheek just under her eye. "I've been offered a job," she says. "A real job. With real pay."

I sit fully upright in about a second. "Wow," I say, and blow out a long breath. "That's pretty amazing."

"It is, rather," says Mom. She takes a sip of tea. "Disgusting. I must have put sugar in both of them."

"You don't look too happy," I say. "If it was me I'd be jumping up and down with delight."

Mom nods. "This is my version of jumping for joy," she says.

"Sorry," I say. "Your jumping for joy looks deceptively like you sitting down in a thoughtful mood."

"I'd still have to do the job." She sips her tea and pulls

a face again. "It's not an easy job, or a fun job, but it's well paid."

"What are you going to do?" I say. "Mud wrestling with alligators or something?"

"Ooh. That is uncanny." Mom sips her tea again. "How did you know?" She takes the cup away and pulls a face. "Actually, it's not quite mud wrestling. I'd be a book-keeper for a big firm of architects."

"So, you haven't accepted it yet?" I say.

"I thought I'd run it by you first," she says.

"Who? Me?" I say.

"No, the table," she says. "It means we wouldn't go back to London. We'd stay here. You could stay in the band. Keep your friends."

"What about Shawn?" I say.

"Sod him." Mom sips her tea. "No. I'm kidding." Sip. "I'd get the car fixed." Sip. "We could go up and see him a couple of times a month. He does actually have two parents. I forget that sometimes."

"If that works for you, then it works for me," I say. "I'm finished with the band, though."

"Sorry to hear that," she says. "Oh. Thanks for the check. But I don't really need it now. That was bad timing. My fault. If I'd known about the job earlier, then I would have stopped you selling Shawn's stuff. Can you go and get it back? Tell the bloke it was a mistake."

"Maybe." I think about the p-bass. I wonder if it's still in the water in Brunswick, or if someone's found it.

Harry might give me my stuff back, but the p-bass is gone. I don't want to spoil Mom's moment so I just say, "Yeah. He's a nice bloke."

"So, I'll call the architects and tell them yes," says Mom.

"If there aren't any jobs working with alligators," I say.

"You, my friend," says Mom as she stands up, "had better get your skates on."

I pull my feet out from under the covers, and sit cross-legged.

"Let's throw a little light on the subject." Mom goes over to the window, takes hold of the curtain, and pulls it back.

I jump several inches off the mattress. There, on the other side of the glass, silhouetted against the rising sun, is the falcon. It glares at me with its amber eyes, spreads its wings, then dives down toward the ocean.

"That was a very grumpy-looking pigeon," says Mom. "I hope it's not a bad sign."

Acknowledgements

I would like to thank the following people for all their help, support, and inspiration while writing this book:

Lisa Jahn Clough, Joanna, Stefan, and Danny Marcus, Mike Bishop, John and Jackie Batten, and Brian Farrey-Latz.

Especial thanks to Rachel Briant of the New York Aquarium for her advice on sharks.

The book is affectionately dedicated to my friend and guitarist, Martin May (1957–2009).

About the Author

Ed Briant grew up in England, but now lives just outside Philadelphia, where he writes, illustrates, and creates the popular comic strip "Tales from the Slushpile." He has two daughters, teaches creative writing, and occasionally plays keyboards with a punk rock band.

Check out his artwork and blog at www.edbriant.com.